January 11, 1973

Barbara Zahn

LOVE WITH HONOR

LOVE WITH HONOR

EMILIE LORING

LITTLE, BROWN AND COMPANY
BOSTON · TORONTO

LIBRARY OF CONGRESS CATALOG CARD NO. 69–15073

FIRST EDITION

Published simultaneously in Canada
by Little, Brown & Company (Canada) Limited

PRINTED IN THE UNITED STATES OF AMERICA

LOVE WITH HONOR

I

SPRING had come back. The last of the snow was gone; the bleak ground was stirring with life; trees that had been like white skeletons all winter were beginning to put out delicate leaves; there was a flush of pale green as underbrush took part in the annual miracle of the resurrection of the earth. The birds were coming back from their southern travels; the light lingered long in the sky. This was the time of renewal, of beginning again.

For Randi Scott the day was to mark the end of the life she had known and to set her feet on a new and completely unforeseen course. But there was no premonition of that in the beginning.

It was the sun that awakened Randi, shining through the green of new leaves on the trees outside her window, lighting the red wash of color on a maple, catching in its beams the scarlet flame of a cardinal that flashed across the deep blue of the sky.

For a moment Randi lay motionless while the dreams of the night faded and the sounds and scents of the spring day took their place. She yawned and stretched, her slender young body as lithe as a cat's. Then she

swung her small feet out of bed and into yellow bedroom slippers, pulled on a matching yellow robe over
her shoulders, and went to stand for a moment looking
out at the tiny garden. All winter it had been snow-
covered, but now it held beds of daffodils like bottled
sunlight and, fragrant hyacinths planted the year before
by her older sister Melody.

Randi felt a familiar ache in her heart. She tried to
shake off the feeling of dread that rarely left her these
days, to remember that the winter had passed safely,
that the warm months lay ahead, the time of planting
and flowering and harvesting. Everything would be all
right for Melody. It had to be all right, she told herself
fiercely. Nonetheless she recalled the words the doctor
had spoken in warning the night before.

"Your sister should not live in this cold, damp climate, Miss Scott. She needs warmth and dry air. In
Arizona or New Mexico she could live a normal,
healthy life. But here — well, you don't need me to tell
you what a rough time she's had."

Randi pushed away the memory. It wasn't words of
caution she needed, it was words of hope to lend courage for the day ahead. She had tried — how she had
tried! — to find some way of moving to the Southwest,
but unless she could sell her small cottage there would
not be enough money to cover their fare and their
living expenses until she could get a job. And there was
no likelihood at all that she would ever find another job
which would pay her half what she was earning on the
one she had gotten a few weeks earlier. Of course she
would save every possible penny.

As so many times in the past she was grateful to her mother, who had taught her the value of poetry in raising and strengthening her thoughts.

"Now is the winter of our discontent made glorious summer," she declaimed to herself, looked out of the window with a brighter face and, after hearing the warning "cuckoo" sound seven times from the little living room clock, hastened to take a shower and dress in her favorite color, a soft daffodil-yellow wool skirt and matching sweater. Her hair was a smooth shining cap of soft black; her eyes were brown with slightly tilted brows beautifully marked, her nose small and straight, her mouth a little too large for beauty, a mouth made for laughter and tenderness. Only the directness of her gaze and the unexpected strength of her chin revealed the character that enabled her to confront life without flinching from responsibility and without self-pity.

For four years, since the death of her parents when she was eighteen, she had supported herself. And now she was supporting her older sister Melody, who, until she fully recovered from rheumatic fever, would be unable to hold a regular job. She had kept their little home going, had provided a housekeeper who could look after Melody as well as prepare the meals, and she had carried the heavy medical expenses that were entailed by Melody's illness.

Up to now Randi felt that she had done the best she could. Increasingly, however, she was torn between Melody's needs and her own love for Willis Jameson, who, as a young lawyer, could not be expected to assume the support of Melody, even if he had ever suggested it. He would not wait forever for her to make her choice and she could not give him up.

Randi drew a long breath, forced herself to smile at her reflection in the mirror, and went across the hall to open the door of her sister's room cautiously.

Melody was awake, her wonderful dark-fringed eyes wide open, their deep blue like the Mediterranean, looking out at the garden. She was so lovely that Randi caught her lip hard between her teeth to hold back tears. Her hair, long and fine as Randi's was dark, covered the pillow like a bright shower of gold. She turned her head quickly and her face lighted up with her gay smile. Life glowed in her like a flickering flame, now bright, now dim, and Randi vowed to herself that whatever the cost, even if it meant losing Willis, she would keep that flame burning.

"You're early!" Melody exclaimed.

"This is Mrs. Echo's late day," Randi reminded her. "She won't be here until ten, and I wanted to have plenty of time to get your breakfast."

There was an odd expression across Melody's face, like the shadow cast by a branch tossed in the wind, and then it was gone so quickly that Randi thought she must have imagined it.

"I suppose she is learning more maxims from her husband," Melody laughed.

The housekeeper's real name was Mrs. Prynne, but the girls referred to her as Mrs. Echo because her conversation consisted largely of quotations from her husband, who, according to her, knew the answer to everything.

When Randi brought up a tray, opened the legs carefully, and set it on the bed, Melody said, "You go down and eat your own breakfast while it is hot."

Randi cleared a small table. "I'll have mine up here with you. You're alone far too much."

Melody gave her sister a quick glance and looked away again. When Randi had brought her own breakfast, Melody asked casually, "How do you enjoy working in the lap of luxury?"

"I don't really work very hard," Randi admitted. "It's not only the highest pay I ever got but the easiest job — and the pleasantest. Mr. King can't dictate more than three hours a day. The rest of the time I do some retyping and, now and then, look up quotations or check dates. Things like that. And some of the time we just talk. I like him."

Melody smiled. "You sound surprised."

"Well," Randi admitted candidly, "I didn't really expect to like him. When Willis told me about the job, you remember, he said that Jonas King was awfully rich, that he was going to write his memoirs to show what a great guy he had been, and that he paid a high salary. Somehow he didn't sound — well, I didn't think he would be so nice."

Again Melody gave her a swift look. "Willis seems to have been mistaken about him."

"Of course," Randi leaped to Willis's defense, "he doesn't know him at all. Just rumor. Actually the book doesn't have anything to do with Mr. King; it's about our past as a nation and how we got that way, and that we must not stop working to keep it that way. And though the house really is the lap of luxury, it's not the money but the beauty you are aware of. It's a — a comfortable sort of place, except that, somehow, it is too dark."

Melody started to speak and then lay back on her bed, in obvious discomfort.

"As soon as I get home this afternoon" Randi said, "I'll call the doctor and ask him to give you a complete checkup."

"Isn't this the night you usually see Willis?" Melody flung out a hand that was almost transparently thin. "Please, Randi, please! You do so much for me. Please keep your date."

There was so much fervent feeling in her voice, almost a kind of desperation, that Randi said, "All right, if you are sure you'll be careful and take care of yourself."

"Today," Melody told her, "I'm going out in the garden. I want to see spring happen."

"You *must* be careful not to get chilled," Randi warned her anxiously.

"If I decide to do some work I'll promise to sit on a cushion so I won't catch cold. Please don't worry about me. I feel such a burden!" It was a cry from the heart. "And I won't be lonely. The Brooks kids from next door will come over as soon as they see me out-of-doors — they always do — and then I'll tell them stories."

ii

In spite of the brilliant sunshine, the forecast had been for rain, and knowing the unpredictability of April days, Randi had put on a lined raincoat. The distance between her small cottage and the King house was less than a mile, but it took her out of the modest middle income group, through the main business street of the village, and beyond into the area of big estates. The village was like the hollow center of a soup plate. On the rise to the north were small homes set on narrow lots. In the center was the village proper, cut in two by Main Street. On the somewhat steeper hill to the south were the lavish establishments of the rich set in ample grounds.

As she walked along Main Street, Randi stopped, as she invariably did, to watch the activities where an office building was being erected, and then edged cautiously past the scaffolding. Just around the corner in a shabby old building Willis Jameson had his office, and occasionally she caught a glimpse of him as he was going into the building. This morning there was no sign of his big, broad-shouldered figure, but the thought of him made her smile in deep contentment. She would see him tonight and that was enough to make the day bright. They would set a date for their wedding. She might even yet achieve her heart's desire and be a June bride. On this spring morning anything seemed possible.

Together she and Willis could work things out financially by combining their incomes. Now that Jonas

King paid her such a high salary, twice what she had ever earned before, they could manage without difficulty. It might be feasible to keep the cottage. If Willis didn't mind, they could live there where Melody could enjoy her garden, the neighborhood children, and Mrs. Echo's kindly if garrulous care.

Then when winter came . . . but whenever she reached that point in her thinking Randi came up against an obstacle. Willis could not pick up and leave the village; her sister could not stay there for another winter; and there was no extra money to send her away and provide for her support.

Beyond Main Street, Randi climbed a steep hill and walked along the great stone wall that enclosed the King estate. To her surprise the heavy, ornate iron gates in the wall stood wide open. She followed the semicircular driveway to the square, three-story stone house. Though it was early in the day for her employer to be having guests — and like most writers he objected strenuously to seeing anyone in the mornings — there was a car parked before the imposing entrance.

The butler, who admitted her, was hastily pulling a jacket over his shirt sleeves. He looked relieved when he saw her. "Oh, Miss Scott! I'm so glad it's you."

"Why?" she asked in surprise. "It's my usual time. Is anything wrong, Luther?"

"It's Mr. King's younger brother, Mr. Hubert. He came in while Mr. King was still having breakfast and barged right up to his room before I could stop him. He's been carrying on something terrible. Making an awful scene. You could hear him shout all over the house. It's bad for Mr. King. He's not supposed to get excited or upset. After that last heart attack the doctor said he was to live like a — like a vegetable."

"I'm surprised that Miss Bertram didn't stop it!" Randi exclaimed. "She usually watches her patient like a hawk."

"I've got my own ideas about that nurse of his," the butler said darkly. "In my opinion —" He broke off as a door at the back of the hall opened and a tall blond woman in a nurse's uniform came toward them. Her hair was artificially tinted, she wore artificial lashes, her makeup must take hours to put on, but the result was effective. In a lush sort of way she was almost beautiful.

She looked quickly from the butler to Randi as though guessing that they had been discussing her.

"Good morning, Miss Scott," she said graciously. "Mr. King is busy. I'm afraid you will have to wait for a while. Do make yourself comfortable."

Mavis Bertram went up the stairs while Randi looked after her. There had been something in the nurse's manner that suggested the mistress of the house addressing a menial rather than one employee speaking to another. Certainly there had been no indication that she was alarmed by the emotional scene to which her patient was being subjected.

The butler's eyes followed the tall blond woman. "If you ask me, she's aiming to be Mrs. King. Well, he's human like the rest of us and she lays on the flattery with a trowel. She may succeed in getting him, after all.

At least I can always find another job. One thing sure, I'd never work for her." He shrugged and went down the hall.

Randi sat on a carved ancient Spanish chair, upholstered in red velvet, and waited. The lap of luxury, Melody had called it. From what she had seen of it, the King house was beautifully appointed and smoothly run. She could hardly blame the nurse if she wanted to make this house her permanent home, from trying to attract Jonas King. Patients often married their nurses. At least, though her motives would be selfish, she would give him good professional care.

It was some time before a door upstairs was flung open and she heard a man shout, ". . . always were pigheaded. No one can talk any sense into you. If you hadn't used undue influence in the first place, Dad would have divided the estate equally between us — he would never have left everything to you. The money. The house."

Randi heard Jonas King's quiet voice reply, "He left you an income for life, Hubert. Twenty thousand a year which you've never had to raise a hand for. You ought to be able to struggle along on that."

"But I can't touch the principal and you won't disgorge a single penny."

"That's right. I won't."

"Just because of that forged check. I was only twenty-five at the time. Just a kid. I didn't know better."

"Twenty-five isn't a child's age. It's a time, if ever, to become a man. And you still don't know better." Jonas's tone was like a whiplash.

"What is that supposed to mean?"

"Do you think I am a fool?" Jonas asked wearily. "You haven't misled me for a moment. You haven't pulled any wool over my eyes. I know what you are up to. I know why you want that money."

"I just want my fair share, that's all."

"You got all Dad thought you had a right to. And you aren't going to lay a hand on a penny of mine, Hubert, to support that new Fascist group — what does it call itself? The All-American Party. Even in politics a man like you can't get anywhere unless he buys his way in. Well, you won't get another cent of the King money, except over my dead body."

There was a curious silence and Randi found herself thinking, in a kind of panic, He shouldn't have said that. He shouldn't have said that.

A door slammed with a crash that made her jump. Sudden shocks like that were dangerous for a man with a bad heart, more dangerous than emotional shocks, but Hubert King didn't seem to care. He ran down the stairs. He was about forty-five, overweight, with a balding head and a round face. His small eyes were set in his face like currants in a piece of unbaked dough. Too angry to be aware of anything but his own emotions, he dashed past Randi without seeing her, flung open the front door and let it bang behind him. A moment later a car door slammed, a motor raced, and then a car rocketed down the driveway, spraying gravel.

Randi went up the wide flight of stairs at the left of the broad entrance hall. Jonas King's library was on the right on the second floor; beyond it were his bedroom, dressing room, and bath, and at the back of the hall was a small elevator that had been installed after his first heart attack.

The library door was open and Randi went in. The blonde nurse was in Jonas's bedroom. From where she stood Randi could see them both. Her employer was the antithesis of his brother. At forty-five Hubert was pudgy, pasty-faced, soft. At fifty, Jonas was gaunt, lean-faced, with a good jaw, alert eyes, and a kindly expression. Mavis had moved very close to him and she was, quite unnecessarily, adjusting his necktie.

With an unexpected gesture of exasperation Jonas detached those clinging hands. "I shan't need you again this morning, Miss Bertram. In fact, as I am having two luncheon guests, you may as well take off the rest of the day. Go out and enjoy this fine weather. I won't need anything."

"How kind you are!" she said in a husky, caressing contralto. "But after that quarrel — it's so bad for you! Wouldn't it be better, Mr. King, to let your brother have what he wants? It would prevent those awful scenes."

"You think it would be better?" he asked curiously.

The artificial lashes fluttered, the heavily rouged mouth smiled. "Oh, of course! You know the doctor said you must have a quiet life. He warned you about excitement and shock. Anyhow, you have so much money you could easily afford to give him what he wants. It isn't as though —"

"As though I would need it long?" he asked oddly. Then he saw the girl in the yellow skirt and sweater hovering uncertainly at the door of the library and he brushed past the nurse.

"Good morning, Miss Scott. Beautiful weather, isn't it?" He added firmly, "That will be all, Miss Bertram."

The nurse hesitated and then went out of the library. Jonas waved Randi to a chair beside his desk and sat down. Then he waited. Several minutes passed before Randi saw a flicker of white and heard the nurse going slowly up the stairs to her own room on the third floor. What on earth had she been doing outside the door all that time?

Then at last Jonas King spoke. "I'd give a lot to be able to get rid of that woman."

"Then why don't you?" Randi asked in astonishment.

"She is my brother's spy," Jonas said quietly. "I knew before she had been here a week that Hubert had planted her in this house."

"But why on earth would he do that?" Randi was shocked and bewildered.

"That's what I want to find out. Hubert has some sort of plan. Poor Hubert *always* has a plan. They practically never work out because he can't see beyond the next move and apparently he can't learn by his mistakes and errors of judgment. And it is obvious to me that for all Miss Bertram's attentive ways," and he grinned in amusement, "that woman is up to something."

"But if you can't trust her — a nurse of all people! — isn't it dangerous to have her here?"

That was the first time the word *danger* was mentioned and it was done almost lightly. After all, at that moment Randi had not yet learned to believe in danger.

"It is better to keep her than to wonder who is replacing her." Jonas King smiled. "You have a most revealing face, Miss Scott. You think I have some sort of persecution complex, don't you?"

She flushed. "No, of course I don't. But, well — it seems so — so melodramatic. And if you distrust her, why should you trust me? After all, I'm a stranger too. You never knew anything about me until I applied for the job less than two months ago."

He laughed outright. "No one could look at you and fail to trust you, Miss Scott." He stretched out his hand for his notes. "Well, shall we go on with the great work?"

II

$\mathscr{A}$S a rule, lunch was served in the library, but today Jonas broke off his dictation to look at the tall clock against the wall and say, "We are having lunch downstairs. I've lent my guesthouse to a young friend of mine, Cary Hamilton, and he is bringing a colleague of his to lunch."

"Cary Hamilton? Is he the one who was on television the other night, talking about the All-American Party and how it is trying to involve schoolchildren?"

"That's the man. I think you will like him."

"I?" Randi was surprised.

"Yes. I hope you will join us, Miss Scott."

For the first time Randi was aware that her employer was studying her, not critically but in an appraising sort of way.

"Thank you. I'd like very much to meet Mr. Hamilton," she said, thinking that the situation was very odd. Mr. King's brother was trying to obtain a position of power in the new Fascist party, which, small as it was, had begun to nibble at the roots of the government, like termites tunneling into a structure until the foundations were undermined. And Mr. King's guest was the most outspoken adversary the party had. For months he had been pointing out the tactics of the enemy within the gates, revealing their lies, challenging their claims, exposing their methods.

Randi wondered whether Hubert King knew of Cary Hamilton's presence in the guesthouse. If he was openly threatening his brother, what was he likely to do to his biggest and strongest enemy?

When Randi had preceded Jonas King out of the tiny elevator they found not only the two young men whom Jonas had asked to lunch but the nurse, who had assumed the role of hostess and was entertaining them with a rather lavish display of charms that were not necessarily a part of a nurse's equipment.

Jonas paused in the doorway and Randi was aware of his anger. Then it was followed by a glimmer of amusement. He motioned for Randi to precede him into the big drawing room. Mavis turned to smile at Jonas, saw Randi, and color flamed in her face, her eyes flashed. Obviously she had not expected that the secretary would be invited to join the luncheon party from which she herself had been so pointedly excluded.

"Hello, Cary." Jonas shook hands with the young man. "I hope you are finding your quarters comfortable. Let me know if they aren't."

"It's wonderful, sir! I can't tell you how much I am enjoying the guesthouse and how grateful I am." Cary Hamilton was even better-looking than he had appeared on the television screen. He was an exceptionally tall man with an open expression, a pleasant baritone voice, and immense vitality.

As Jonas made a gesture of discomfort at his thanks, Cary changed the subject quickly. He introduced his colleague, John Lancing.

The other man was smaller and slighter than Cary, with hair so blond it seemed almost white, and a plain face that was transformed by his delightful smile.

"I trust, Mr. King," he said, "you won't feel that I am imposing on your hospitality."

"I'm not being hospitable," Jonas said, "I'm being extremely crafty. I hope you'll stay on as long as you can. I want Cary to regard the place as his own home. In fact, I want him to get used to it, make it a permanent address where he can put down roots."

Lancing flashed his engaging smile. "Cary will probably have to be torn away by sheer force from what I've seen of his reaction to the place. But while he could possibly put up with me for a while, I have a small son who is a bit strenuous, to put it mildly. People generally prefer to take Andy in small doses."

Jonas presented the two young men to Randi. "Wasn't I lucky to get a secretary like this?" he said.

Mavis gave Randi a furious look. There was so much jealousy and resentment in it that Randi was startled. Unknowingly she had made an enemy of this woman, and she was aware that the nurse could be a bad enemy.

For a moment, as Cary Hamilton's fingers closed over Randi's hand in a warm clasp, she was startled to find his eyes regarding her as though he recognized her with an astonished kind of delight. She drew away her hand with an effort and turned to greet his friend.

When they entered the dining room, Jonas observed

that the table had been set for four. Mavis had been very sure of herself or else she had intended, by sheer effrontery, to take her place among his guests, because she was waiting, her manner almost challenging.

"Thank you very much for looking after my guests, Miss Bertram, until Miss Scott was free to take over." Jonas smiled blandly at the nurse's baffled face, and she went out of the room.

An irrepressible grin widened the butler's mouth at the woman's discomfiture, and then his face resumed its usual look of bland impassivity.

For a few minutes the conversation was general. Then, as Jonas began to question Cary about his work, Lancing turned eagerly to the pretty girl beside him. They talked gaily as though they were old friends, but all the time Randi was acutely aware of the tall young man who was listening to their host. Something about him seemed to compel her attention. Intuitively she felt that though his eyes were on Jonas King's face, he was as conscious of her as she was of him.

To her surprise she realized that she had never had this — this sharp awareness — of Willis, though they had been engaged for two years. For a moment she was troubled by a sense of disloyalty and then she was amused at herself. In another three months she and Willis would be married; she was unlikely ever to meet Mr. Hamilton again except in the most casual way. He was, without doubt, the most attractive and vital man she had ever encountered, but after all, Willis was Willis.

Once Lancing broke off in the relation of a very

funny story he was telling her to listen as there was a
shriek of rage outdoors. He half rose in his chair. Then
he subsided, saying apologetically, "That's my off-
spring acting up. Sometimes I wonder — I never meant
to spoil him, but since my wife died a year ago he has
got completely out of hand. The women I hire to look
after him always seem to spoil him hopelessly because
he is such an attractive kid. They let him have his own
way about everything."

Seeing Randi's half smile he said, "That's not just
parental bias." He took out his wallet, flipped it open to
two facing pictures. One was a four-year-old boy with
tight blond curls, red cheeks, blue eyes, and his father's
bewitching smile.

"Oh," Randi breathed, enraptured, "what a little
cherub!"

"You see," the cherub's father said in resignation,
"women simply drool. They let him get away with
murder; they can't seem to say no. The result is that a
basically nice child is being ruined."

Randi looked at the facing picture for a long time.

"That was my wife Helen," Lancing said quietly.

Randi handed back the picture. "She makes me think
of my sister Melody; the same coloring, the same
general type."

"Helen was — rather special," Lancing said. "If she
had lived, Andy would be a happy, disciplined child,
instead of the unscrupulous little show-off he has become, screaming for everything he wants."

Randi looked across the table to find Cary's eyes on
her face, to see that Jonas King was watching the

progress of the conversation between her and Lancing with unexpected interest. Again she had the curious impression that her employer was weighing her in the balance.

Cary, glancing at his watch, exclaimed, "Sorry! I know we must not keep you too long. I forgot you were working on a book. How is it progressing?"

Jonas smiled deprecatingly. "I suspect that it is therapy rather than literature but it fills the time. I haven't attempted anything important. A small book, a kind of primer of the past, to remind people of the values on which we are built, the magnificent way we built them, the growing need to maintain them."

"In a world that is discarding values, that prefers violence as a shortcut to justice, and demonstrating as a substitute for intelligent thought, I can't imagine anything more important," Cary declared.

"Your work is more important," Jonas told him. "I'm trying to remind people of our values, but you are helping to maintain them. I'm behind you all the way."

Cary smiled. "That is good to know, sir. We're going to need all the support we can get."

"What's your worst problem?"

"Apathy," Cary replied promptly and Lancing nodded his agreement. "People want our country to continue to be democratic, but they don't try to keep it so, they don't work at it, they don't stop the attempts to undermine us. We have to be alert all the time. We can't sit back and say, 'Too bad, but it doesn't concern me.' The group of high-school kids organized to demonstrate against their schools or their courts of law or their government, end, over and over, in acts of violence deliberately whipped up. Little things, but they matter. They add up." Cary checked himself. "Sorry, sir. That's my hobbyhorse."

When he had thanked his host for his hospitality, he turned to Randi. "So we are really going to be neighbors," he said. "That is nice to know; it rounds out a perfect lunch." He took her hand, smiled down at her, and then the two guests took their leave.

After Randi and Jonas had returned to the library, the latter dictated for an hour in a desultory sort of way, as though his mind were not on what he was saying, and then he pushed aside his notes, waved away the script Randi had prepared for him, and sat brooding while she typed busily at her desk, which had been arranged in a corner of the library.

Above the desk there was an old Federalist mirror that reflected the open door of the library and a bit of the staircase. Several times she was aware of the nurse's silent approach or caught a glimpse of her white uniform as she went noiselessly up and down the stairs. Miss Bertram had not chosen to take advantage of her patient's suggestion that she go out. In a way there was something ridiculous about the way the woman hovered. What on earth did she imagine they were discussing in the library? Somehow, Jonas King's conviction that she was his brother's spy did not seem quite so absurd as it had when he had first spoken of it that morning.

Jonas's quiet voice broke in on her thoughts. "What is so fascinating out of the window?"

"Spring," Randi said, her eyes on the forsythia. "Blossoms coming and spring happening, and sunshine."

" 'You came and the sun came after,' " he quoted unexpectedly. As she turned startled eyes on him he said, "Randi, I want you to marry me."

ii

For a moment she was too bewildered to answer. The idea that Jonas King, a millionaire several times over, nearly thirty years her senior, and an invalid, had suddenly asked her to become his wife was more than she could absorb.

Seeing her stunned expression, Jonas smiled. "I would like to explain my position and then I would like you to think very carefully about it before you give me an answer. I don't want to rush you into anything. And in any case, you are not to imagine that if you refuse me you will jeopardize your position in any way or find it awkward for you to the slightest extent. I shall always want you to stay here, in whatever capacity you prefer."

"But —" Randi began.

He held up his hand to forestall what she had to say. "Wait." For a moment he leaned back in his big black leather chair, as though garnering strength, and then he straightened up. "It's important that there should be no misunderstanding. I am not asking you to be my wife in any literal sense. I am a sick man with a tired heart. A very tired heart. I may live a few years — with luck. I may live only a few months; perhaps only a few weeks."

"Mr. King!"

He shook his head emphatically. "No, no. I don't want your sympathy. Death and I are familiar companions. We are almost old friends. I am prepared for what will happen and I can accept it without regrets. But I don't want either — let's say — to hasten the end unnecessarily."

"I don't understand."

He sat staring at his hands while Randi stared at him, a man who had, until a few short weeks ago, been a stranger to her. She had known of him, of course, because of his wealth and prominence and the beauty of his estate. But the man himself had been only a legend. It was a good face, worn with suffering but unembittered, compassionate, understanding, imaginative, highly intelligent.

He raised his head at last. "This is a hard thing to say, Randi, but my brother Hubert wants me out of the way. He wants my money and sometimes — increasingly often — I am fairly sure that he is not willing to wait for it until my death."

"Oh, no!" Randi cried out in horror, her eyes wide with shock.

"There are times," Jonas said, "when I have been on the verge of turning over the bulk of my estate to Hubert, because money and power are so terribly important to him, but, Randi, I can't do it. I can't justify it to my conscience just to secure my own safety. I've been watching Hubert's activities for a long time. He is one of the local leaders of the All-American Party that is trying, among other things, to propagandize our children in the schools, trying to make them believe that democracy does not work, that the Bill of Rights is vicious nonsense, that the Supreme Court is corrupt or controlled by the Communists, or some such outrageous nonsense, that the individual must become part of an organized mob led by suitable people. Himself, for example."

Randi had heard too much of the underground movement to doubt its potential for evil.

"Hubert's method," Jonas went on, "is not like that of Cary Hamilton, who fights just about everything my brother represents. Cary stands for straightforward dealing; Hubert prefers to work underground, to burrow."

Jonas hesitated. "It is not too much to say that what is going on today is a battle, a new kind of battle, a battle for the minds not only of the adults but of the children of this country. Books that take a different stand from that advocated by these enemies of the government disappear from the schools, or are mutilated in the libraries, or vanish from the shelves in bookstores. People like that fear free speech, of course, and the free use of the mind."

Again he leaned back to rest. Then he went on. "One of these days Hubert may succeed in his attempts to bring about another heart attack — and that is what he was after this morning — unless —" He met Randi's eyes squarely. "Unless I were to make sure that he would have nothing to gain by hastening my — uh — departure. I intend to draw up a new will, of course, excluding him entirely, but there is no telling — with the unscrupulous forces behind him, he might be able to persuade the courts that he had been tricked. So I want to be married; I want my wife to have a right to claim my estate."

"But I —" Randi paused. "Mr. King, I couldn't take your money. It wouldn't be fair."

He smiled. "My idea would be to provide you with an adequate income for life." He added casually, "That would enable you to give your sister the care she needs; especially to make her completely independent of you, which is the greatest boon you could confer."

"Independent?" Randi's eyes were wide with bewilderment.

"I know by experience," Jonas said, "that even the most loving care can be stifling, particularly if one thinks it is accompanied by self-sacrifice." He grinned with sudden wry humor. "Self-sacrifice is more blessed to give than to receive."

"I hadn't thought of that," Randi admitted. "Perhaps I have sort of — smothered Melody by too much anxiety."

"Well, then," Jonas went on briskly, "to get on to the main thing. I mean to leave this house and the bulk of my estate to the King Foundation, of which Cary will be the director. If anyone can succeed in fighting the forces that are trying to seduce our people away from the American system, he is the one. I feel sure,

beyond the shadow of a doubt, that you would see my
wishes are carried out. The fact that you, as my widow,
supported the Foundation would convince the courts
that I had been completely aware of what I wanted done
and that I was responsible for my own actions.

"What I am offering you, Randi, is a marriage of
convenience, for us both. It would help you to help your
sister; it would help me to prolong my life; it would
prevent the King money from being used for an evil
purpose. In any case, it would bring sunlight into this
house, make life brighter, and drive away some of the
shadows."

A slight movement made Randi look quickly in the
mirror. There was a flicker of white and then quiet
footsteps moving away. She looked back at Jonas and
started to speak, but he put his finger to his lips in
warning and then noiselessly shaped the question, "Is it
the nurse?"

She nodded.

When a door closed in the distance he said in a tone
of amusement, "I wonder just how long it will be before Hubert is informed that I intend to be married."

"Mr. King —"

"Well, Randi?" His voice was gentle.

"I can't marry you. I'm proud to think that you
would ask me, but I can't."

"Why not?" he asked, still in that gentle tone. "You
understand, don't you, that I would expect nothing of
you but your presence in my house, taking over the
duties of hostess. I saw today at luncheon how well you
can do that."

"Is that why you were watching me?" she asked in surprise.

He gave a curious little smile. "That is one reason."

"I am sorry," she said again. "You see, it's out of the question, because I am engaged to be married."

There was a long pause and then Jonas said, "I didn't know that. Who is this fortunate young man?"

"His name is Willis Jameson. He's a lawyer who is just getting started on his career."

Jonas smiled. "And you are very much in love?"

Randi smiled back. "Very much."

"Have you been engaged long?"

"Two years."

"Two years!" His expression had changed ludicrously.

"Well, he is just starting out, as I said." Unexpectedly Randi felt, in the light of the older man's astonishment, that she had to defend Willis. "He can't afford to support a wife yet. If I could add my salary to his we would be able to manage easily, but — there's my sister. He felt I should make — a choice, but I think I've convinced him we could work things out easily. I think maybe, if everything goes well, we could be married in June. I guess every girl dreams of being a June bride."

"I see." Jonas turned his big chair away, and sat staring at the magnificent Renoir on the wall, which glowed against the background of the dark rows of leatherbound books. When he turned again, he was smiling at the girl's anxious expression. "Suppose we leave the whole thing in abeyance for the time being. But remember — the offer stands."

III

$\mathscr{A}$ LIGHT rain was falling when Randi left Jonas King's house. As usual he offered her the use of his car; as usual she refused it. She preferred to walk; she enjoyed the exercise. Anyhow, on Wednesday evenings she met Willis, and it was hardly tactful to expect Jonas whom she had refused to marry to provide transportation to take her to Willis whom she had accepted.

She walked slowly, thinking about that startling interview with Jonas. He wanted to marry her, to make her the mistress of the splendid King house during his lifetime and to leave her an income for life. The idea was so momentous that she could hardly grasp it. Not for a moment did she contemplate accepting his offer, of course. Marriage was more than a matter of mutual convenience; it was a sacrament. Anyhow, there was Willis.

She thought of the nurse who, Jonas believed, was his brother's spy; who, the butler believed, intended to become Mrs. Jonas King. If she had overheard Jonas's proposal, as seemed likely, Mavis Bertram must be furious. She had been angry enough when Randi had taken over as hostess at lunch.

Randi walked on more slowly. There was also

Jonas's unstressed comment that such a marriage would provide him with a measure of safety, might even prolong his life. As it might insure Melody's complete recovery. Randi had come to a halt now, torn between conflicting loyalties. And then she shook her head. A marriage that was no marriage — there was no excuse for it. She hastened on, her step lighter now she was sure in her own mind that she had made the right decision. She was almost running when she reached the two-story building off Main Street in which Willis had his office above a watch repair shop. Looking up from the street, she saw that the lights in the insurance office next door were being switched off but that Willis's lights still burned. He was waiting for her, of course.

Her warm tender lips curved in a smile. They would have dinner at a quiet inn in the next village where, during midweek, there were few diners and they could talk at leisure. They would set a date for their wedding and make plans. At long last they would make plans. The trouble with Willis was that when you wanted to be serious he found something to laugh about, to turn everything into a joke, and then somehow the evening had faded away and there was no time left for planning. Next time, he vowed, they would really settle down to it.

Randi went up the dusty and rickety stairs to the second floor. The door of the insurance office was being locked by a sandy-haired girl, who nodded to Randi.

"She's still in there," she said in an odd voice and went down the stairs with the light step of one released from bondage.

She? Willis had a stenographer who worked mornings, as he could not yet afford a full-time employee. He rarely saw a client this late in the afternoon.

Randi opened the door hesitantly for fear of interrupting a conference between lawyer and client. Then she stood as motionless as though she had been turned to stone. Willis was beside his desk, his back to her. His head was bent as he kissed the woman he had crushed in his arms. All Randi could see of her was the hand that pressed against his shoulder, a hand wearing a magnificent square-cut emerald ring that blazed in the light.

After an eternity Randi backed out of the shabby office and closed the door behind her as noiselessly as she could.

ii

In her state of shock she stumbled against the DANGER sign on the sidewalk where the building was being erected. It was the first time she had failed to stop in fascination to watch its progress. Every step, from the digging of the excavation, had been exciting. Building things! That was what America was all about.

"Hey, watch it, lady!" a policeman yelled, and she looked up, startled, to the cumbersome staging directly overhead. "Can't you read?" the policeman added. "You want a bucket of cement on your head or to have one of these ropes break, maybe, and send the whole business down on you?"

"Sorry." She stepped out into the street and skirted the building.

Willis! For a moment she almost turned to go back to his office. There must be some mistake, some explanation. Why, after an engagement of two years, was he kissing another girl? If he loved someone else, why hadn't he told her? She would never have attempted to hold him without his love. He must know that.

How long had another girl been so important in his life? There had never been the slightest hint that he was interested in anyone else. True, he avoided any attempts at serious talk, at planning for the wedding, but she had taken his attitude for a boyish casualness. What a fool she had been!

She wondered when he would realize that she was not going to keep her appointment that night. Sooner or later, he was bound to discover that she was not coming. Unless, indeed, he had forgotten her very existence. She blinked tears. Tonight they had intended to make plans for their wedding. They? *She* had intended to make plans. No doubt, Willis would have laughed, have changed the subject, have discovered some new reason for delay. Her face burned as she realized how long he had been amusing himself at her expense.

Randi straightened her shoulders, held her head high. She would never let him know how deeply he had hurt her.

As she entered the cottage she heard Mrs. Echo's tireless voice. "Well, as my husband always says, it's not just living to eat, it's eating to live. Like a bird. That's the way you eat. Like a bird. You hardly touched your lunch. Miss Randi is going to be upset, I can tell you."

"Please don't mention it to Randi, Mrs. Prynne. Please don't. You'd only worry her."

The housekeeper heard the urgent plea in the girl's voice. "Don't you fret yourself, Miss Melody. Like my husband always says, least said, soonest mended."

"Randi!" Melody exclaimed in surprise. "I thought you were going to have dinner with Willis tonight."

"Not tonight."

Something in Randi's face and her lifeless voice silenced the questions on Melody's lips.

"You might as well go, Mrs. Prynne," Randi said. "I'll be here all evening."

The housekeeper's face lighted. "Well, I must say that's real nice of you and I'll make up the time whenever you like. There's a good nourishing casserole in the refrigerator. All you need to do is heat it up. And there's lettuce and cucumbers for a salad."

Still talking, she put on her coat, gathered up her umbrella, and went out. Together the girls, the dark and the fair, stood at the window and watched her square, vigorous body bobbing down the street under a big umbrella.

"She looks like a mushroom, if you can imagine a mushroom in locomotion." Melody laughed, gave her sister a quick, anxious look, and turned back to the window. She had been worried by Randi's unexpected return; fearing, as she had so often in recent months, that her younger sister was sacrificing one of her few opportunities for pleasure in order to stay with her. But something more than that had brought Randi home on a night when she usually met Willis. Something had drained the color from her face and left her eyes wide with shock.

Sunk in her thoughts, Randi was unaware of her sister's troubled expression. She was not aware of the April shower or that the light was beginning to fade from the sky. She saw only that one incredible picture of Willis holding a girl in his arms, and the girl's hand, white against the dark shoulder of his coat, a big emerald blazing in the light.

Willis whom she had loved and promised to marry. Willis who, she had assumed, returned her love. Of course, their engagement had been vague from the outset. He couldn't marry yet, he had admitted. He knew he was selfish to hold her to an engagement, when he had so little to offer, but he couldn't bear the thought of her marrying anyone else. So the engagement had dragged on, month after month. Now and then, they had made tentative wedding plans but always had to postpone them because of some unexpected obstacle. Not yet. Not yet.

There were times when Randi found the lengthy engagement difficult to explain to her friends. More difficult times when her friends pointed to young couples who had married on less money than Willis made and who were managing well. There were friends who even hinted that Randi was expecting too much, that she was not willing to settle for a modest income, that it was she who kept the devoted Willis dangling after her.

And always, and worst of all, there had been Mel-

ody's ominous and eloquent silence about Willis. The
sisters knew each other too well to deceive each other,
but Randi knew that Melody was disturbed by that long
engagement, that she distrusted Willis and doubted
that he returned Randi's devotion.

Melody had left the window to lie on the couch.
Randi immediately snapped out of her preoccupation
with her own troubles. "Tired?" she asked, and could
have bitten off her tongue when she saw the shadow
cross Melody's face. Jonas King had been right. She
was oppressing her beloved sister by too much obvious
care.

"No, I had fun today," Melody said cheerfully. "I
was out of doors every single minute I could be until it
began to sprinkle. I did some weeding and planted the
annuals. They should have gone in before now, of
course, but the ground was frozen so long this year.
Ugh! What a brutal winter! But it's over now. And the
Brooks youngsters came over and were as enchanting
as usual and I told them stories. I wish —" She broke
off.

"Wait until I get that casserole out of the refrigerator to take off the chill before I put it in the oven."
When Randi had removed the casserole, mixed a salad,
and put the salad bowl in the refrigerator to cool, she
came back to drop onto a chair beside the couch. "What
do you wish, Melody?"

"I wish I could do more things. All day I've been
thinking about it. There's no real reason now why I
can't get the meals and do everything except, perhaps,

the laundry and the heavy cleaning. It isn't good for us, either for you or for me, to have me begin to feel like an invalid. I'm not really one. The less I try to do the less I'll be able to do. And I wish there was some way I could earn money! I wouldn't be such a burden to you!" Melody burst out.

"*You* a burden? You know better." Randi dropped down beside the couch and for a moment the sisters clung together, each providing what comfort she could. Then Randi settled back in her chair, blinking tears from her lashes. She remembered again what Jonas King had said, and tried to put herself in Melody's position. Never before had she realized how much more difficult Melody's role was than her own, always to be taken care of, always to be receiving instead of giving.

"You know, Melody, you may have something there. That is, if you'd really like to earn some money."

"*If!*" It was a cry from the heart.

"Well, we can start by having you get lunch, say. Then dinner. Then doing the straightening up. Only, of course, you should ease into it gradually."

"Of course." There wasn't much eagerness in Melody's voice, only acquiescence.

"What would really make you happy?" Randi asked.

Melody did not need a moment's thought about that. "I get along well with children. I love them and I think they know it, but I don't spoil them and they obey me. I've been thinking perhaps I could set up some sort of prekindergarten school where working mothers could send their youngsters."

Randi sat bolt upright, her eyes shining. "It's an idea, Melody! A marvelous idea. Children adore you. I don't see why it shouldn't work, if you don't find it too strenuous."

"Well, of course, we'd need some equipment and toys and — I was thinking that if you don't mind eating in the kitchen, we could clear out the dining room and use that — and —"

"Whoa!" Randi laughed. "You are going too fast."

Some of the brightness faded. "Of course. I forgot. It would probably cost quite a bit to get started, remodeling the cottage, getting equipment, advertising —"

"It's not that. I was thinking of another possibility. Today at lunch I met a man named John Lancing, a widower with a small boy. I saw a picture of him and he's a cherub, simply adorable, but according to his father he has become so spoiled since his mother died that he is turning into a problem child."

"What a pity! What a waste!"

"If you could look after someone like that, give him training in self-restraint and respect for other people and teach him how to get along with them before it's too late, find out what his own talents are and help him to develop them, it might be more useful than dealing with a number of children, and having to spread thin the personal attention you could give each one."

"I'd love to try it," Melody said wistfully. Then her eyebrows arched in surprise. "At lunch, you said? Do you mean Old Moneybags asked you to lunch?"

"Please, Melody, don't speak of Mr. King like that."

There was an unusual touch of sharpness in Randi's voice. "He's a very nice person, a very fine person, sensitive and perceptive and understanding."

"That," Melody replied with a touch of tartness in her usually soft voice, "is not my name for the man. It's what Willis called him when he spoke about the job in the first place."

"Yes, I know." As the telephone shrilled beside her, Randi started to put out her hand to silence it, and then let her hand drop. It was long past the time when she had been due at Willis's office. Apparently the girl with the emerald ring had gone and he had remembered her. He was beginning to wonder what made her so late.

The telephone rang five times, ten times, broke off in the middle of the eleventh ring.

"What's wrong, Randi?" Melody demanded. "Something happened today, didn't it?"

"Yes," Randi admitted. "Something happened. A lot of things happened."

"And you aren't going to see Willis tonight?"

"I'm not going to see Willis — ever," Randi said crisply. She pushed back her chair. "I'd better turn on the oven."

The telephone rang again while they were eating their dinner and a third time while they sat in the darkened living room looking out at a crescent moon, which seemed to be snared on the branch of a tree. It was some time later when car lights flashed across the windows and were switched off. For a few minutes the familiar shabby Volkswagen waited in front of the house with Willis at the wheel. Apparently from the fact that the house was dark and the telephone unanswered, he assumed that there was no one at home and he had decided to await their return. Not that he would wait long. Willis was an impatient man who could not endure delays, except — except, Randi thought bitterly, when it came to marriage.

She could picture how he looked, sitting there, a long lock of hair falling over his eyes, lips smiling, preparing one of his endless jokes, his face engaging in its boyishness. Once when she had said, laughing, that she was afraid it would be years before he would look old enough to be taken seriously as a lawyer, Willis had shaken his head.

"You are mistaken about that. Actually, it is an asset. I look so darned young and naïve and inexperienced that it puts people off. Now and then it is a sound idea, it definitely pays, to have people underestimate you. When you come up with something good, they are thrown off balance. I've seen it work in court."

Randi had joined in his laughter, but the comment had obscurely troubled her and she had tried to brush it away, to forget it. Willis hadn't really meant it. Just another of his lighthearted jokes.

After a few minutes, as she had expected, Willis switched on the car radio. He could not endure silence. There was a burst of loud dance music. Then, after some twenty minutes of waiting, the Volkswagen moved away. At least, Willis had waited ten minutes longer than she had expected. Apparently it mattered to him that she had not kept her appointment with him at his office.

When Randi was sure that he was not coming back she drew the draperies and put on the lights. She was very pale.

"You know I don't make a habit of interfering." Melody broke the silence that hung uneasily over the two girls, unusual silence because as a rule they chattered away constantly. "You said a lot of things happened today." She waited, afraid to approach any nearer to the subject of Willis and what appeared to be a broken engagement.

"You've never liked Willis, have you?" Randi asked.

"Well, I — there's nothing really — if you love him that's the important —" Melody stumbled in her attempt to be truthful without hurting her sister.

"Why don't you like him?"

Recognizing this as an honest demand for truth, Melody said, "I've always thought he was unreliable. I've never quite —"

"Trusted him?" Randi asked steadily.

"Well, I couldn't see why he didn't marry you two years ago when you first got engaged. I've never understood what all this delay was about. You wouldn't have cared how little money he earned. You're like me. If he had a hamburger stand you'd be satisfied and willing to help him cook hamburgers, as long as they were *good* hamburgers. So I was afraid he was — just stringing you along and I couldn't figure it out. You're so sweet, Randi, and so trusting. By setting up an engagement —

and he never even bought you a ring, though he got himself those onyx cuff links and that black-pearl tiepin — he kept other men away from you and held the prettiest girl in town at his beck and call without committing himself."

"In other words, you didn't really believe he loved me?" When Melody made a helpless gesture instead of answering, Randi said coolly, "You were right."

She described the scene on which she had stumbled in Willis's office. "I couldn't see the girl, just that fabulous emerald she was wearing. But the way he held her — he was never in love with me like that. Only I can't understand him. In that case, why did he set up that fiction of an engagement? Obviously he has been mad about another woman all this time, or at any rate he certainly is now."

"Do you think he is mad about her — really? Or does she have a lot of money?" Melody asked shrewdly.

"You think that would matter so much?" When Melody made no reply, Randi said slowly, "I don't know anything about her except that she was wearing a ring that would keep us in clover for a long, long time, and Willis couldn't possibly have bought it."

Melody shook her head in perplexity. "What I can't understand, if he didn't intend to marry you, is why he went to the trouble of telling you about that job with Mr. King and urging you to apply for it. I thought he wanted you to make that big salary so that — well, frankly, so you could help support the family when you married him. Not that you would have minded. But now —" Melody stopped short, looking at her sister's shocked face. "Randi! What is it?"

Randi stared at her, stunned by the possibility that had occurred to her. How had Willis learned that Jonas King, whom he did not know, with whom he had no possible association, was in need of a secretary? Why had he wanted her to take that job?

She waited for a moment because her thoughts were in a whirl. "I told you other things had happened today." She described that strange interview she had had with Jonas King in which he had asked her to marry him. She made as faithful a report as she could, with one omission. She did not say that Jonas had suggested that she could help her sister by making such a marriage. Melody would hate that.

"Well," Melody said on a long breath when she had finished, "you meant it when you said things had been happening. Of all the incredible — Randi, do you think Mr. King is in his right mind?"

Randi burst out laughing and Melody, who had been alarmed by her set expression, was relieved.

"Thanks for the compliment! One thing I am sure of — he is the sanest person I know."

"But that his own brother would want to — to get rid of him for his money — I can't believe it."

"You haven't seen the brother and heard him shouting and banging doors. And you haven't watched that nurse skulking around, trying to listen to what we say."

"You really think the brother may have planted her in the house to see what was going on?"

"I think it is probable, but of course I don't know for sure. But I did hear her try to persuade Mr. King to give his brother what he wants. She told him it would be for his own protection; it would prevent any more of those frightful scenes. And she implied that, anyhow, he wouldn't need money much longer."

"Randi! How beastly."

"She's a beastly woman, though very attractive. And I suspect that she is trying to help herself as well as brother Hubert. There are two strings to her bow. Today she attempted to set herself up as his hostess, to establish herself in such a way that she would force him to ask her to lunch, and Mr. King put a stop to it so fast it made her head swim."

"And then," Melody said with a smile, "he asked you to take on the job instead."

Randi laughed. "It made her simply furious with me."

"And do you think that brother Hubert is really involved in the All-American Party?"

"I'm afraid so. And you know what those people are like; they need money to finance their propaganda. Mr. King is determined they shan't use his for such an ugly purpose. That, of course, as I explained, is why he made the proposal he did."

"You haven't," Melody said at last, "told me how you answered Mr. King's proposal."

"I said," Randi replied, "that I was engaged to be married." She began to laugh and the laugh turned to a sob. Stumbling, she ran up the stairs to her room.

Long after she had turned out the reading light beside her bed she lay staring into the dark. The girl who had awakened to sunshine and spring that morning, who had looked ahead to planning her wedding, now listened to the monotonous drum of rain on the roof and brooded over the future. Willis had been playing some kind of game with her. She wondered who the girl with the emerald would be. Oddly enough, she felt neither jealousy nor resentment, only surprise. And she wondered again how Willis had known that Jonas King would want a secretary and why he had urged her to apply for the job. She remembered Jonas's unexpected proposal of marriage.

"The offer stands," he had said when she left him.

The offer stands. But he had not made an appeal to her sympathy, he had not stressed the safety she might help him achieve by marrying him. A marriage of convenience. Mutual convenience.

She tossed restlessly, turned the pillow, and turned away from the memory of Willis with a girl in his arms.

And suddenly the picture faded, making way for a curiously vivid recollection of Cary Hamilton smiling down at her, her hand clasped in his. It was odd, she thought, as she drifted off to sleep, that the only happening of the day she had failed to report to her sister was her meeting with Cary Hamilton. She had mentioned John Lancing and his son and the work he was doing. She had not said a word about Cary Hamilton.

IV

FOUR times during the night Randi was awakened by the sound of Melody tossing and turning in the next room, so she was relieved, when she had dressed for the day, eyes shadowed but tearless in spite of the sudden ending of her two-year absorption in Willis Jameson, to find that her sister was still asleep.

Mrs. Echo was bustling around the kitchen when she went downstairs. "I sure was glad to get off early last night, Miss Randi. My husband is working on that new building on Main Street. He was on the staging when it tipped to one side; the ropes went slack or something, and he nearly took a spill. He could of broke an arm or a leg. He's got a real shiner this morning. Thank goodness, the building won't be more than four stories tall. I don't know how other wives feel but I wouldn't have an easy moment if my husband was working twenty to forty stories up in the air. Especially where there is no proper supervision. That rope should never have slipped. They ought to check more carefully before they send men up. Like my husband always says, a stitch in time saves nine."

Randi closed the front door quietly after her so as not

to awaken her sleeping sister and stepped off the porch onto the sidewalk. She stopped short as Willis, who had been leaning against a porch pillar, took her arm and fell into step beside her as she walked down the street.

"What happened to you last night?" he asked abruptly. "I waited and waited at the office. I kept calling you. Finally I came here but you weren't home. What happened to you and where did you go without telling me?"

Randi's heart was pounding but she was surprised to hear how calm her own voice sounded. "That doesn't really concern you, does it, Willis?"

His hand tightened on her arm so that she jerked it away, exclaiming, "Stop it! You are hurting me."

"What do you mean — it doesn't concern me? The girl I am going to marry stands me up without a word of explanation and then says it doesn't concern me."

"The girl you are going to marry? No, Willis, that is all over."

He gripped her arm again, turned her so that she faced him, saw the blazing light in his eyes. "I demand an explanation. A man has a right to expect the girl he is going to marry —"

"I'm not going to marry you, Willis. That's final, irrevocable."

"When I saw you Saturday night everything was as usual. Then, without warning, out of a clear sky, for no reason at all, you throw me off. That's not like you, Randi. Why didn't you come to meet me at the office last night?"

They were still facing each other, and there was an answering spark of anger in Randi's clear brown eyes. "Oh, I did come, Willis," she said gently. "The trouble was not that I was too late, it was that I came too early, before you expected me. I found you busy. Very busy."

The color drained out of his face and then came back in a flood. "What does that mean?"

She shrugged and started to walk on again so that he was forced to accompany her. "You know as well as I do," she said wearily, "that I found another girl in your office. Or, to be quite accurate, in your arms. So I went home. There didn't seem to be any place for me in your office or in your life."

Willis bit his lip. "Look here, Randi, I admit that must have surprised you." He seemed rather taken aback by her sudden burst of laughter.

"That," she said, "is one way of putting it."

"I can explain the whole thing. This woman — you saw her?" There was something odd in his voice, something strained in his expression.

"Just that ring she was wearing, with a great big emerald."

Willis's face relaxed. "It was a weird situation," he said, talking quickly, improvising as he went. "Quite embarrassing, in fact. The poor girl —"

"Poor? With that ring?"

"Money isn't everything," Willis said in such a chiding tone that Randi nearly laughed again. "The ring was a present from her husband. He died recently and there has been some legal problem about his estate.

His brother has tried to claim that she used undue influence in getting him cut out of the will. All that sort of nonsense. I just happened to be able to clear things up for her and she was — uh — well, you know how emotional women are. She was grateful and excited and she just threw her arms around me as a kind of thank you."

Randi laughed. "You mean you were more kissed against than kissing."

Willis flushed and Randi remembered that he did not like being laughed at. "It doesn't seem like you to be jealous," he said.

"I'm not jealous," she answered truthfully. "I'm just — finished, Willis."

"If I could just make you understand how it was," he insisted, "you would see that you are making a mountain out of a molehill."

"Look here, Willis, I don't believe a single word of that ridiculous story. We are *finished*. And really, I can't see why you even want to bother to try to patch things up with me, as things are."

"We *can't* be finished! Nothing has changed."

"Everything has changed." Her voice was crisp. There was no sign of yielding about her face.

"Then the change is in you, not in me. Darling," he said, giving her the boyish smile that had so attracted her, "you know how I adore you."

She shook her head. "Sorry, Willis, it just doesn't work any more."

They walked on in deep silence for a few minutes.

Then Willis, who had been stealing quick looks at her face, his own growing more sullen, said abruptly, "I think I can see how it really is, Randi. I still have my way to make and a long way to go. I can't offer you a luxurious life and a big house and all the advantages that come with marrying a rich man."

"What makes you think I'll marry a rich man?" she asked.

"Why — well, of course, I always have known I had a lot of competition. I guess I expected too much of you, thinking you would be able to wait, that you would settle for the little I have to offer."

"I'm amazed at you!" she said angrily. "For the past two years, I'd have married you in a minute if you had really wanted me to."

"Wanted!"

She stopped him with a gesture. "I didn't care how much money you had. I was willing — glad — to work and contribute to the finances. You know all that. You've always known it. Let's not add dishonesty to this situation. I'd rather have a clean break and no bitterness. Now let's forget each other, forget we were ever engaged, forget that I ever believed I loved you."

"Dishonesty," he said slowly. "Randi, if we must speak in such terms, can you swear to me that you are not turning me down so that you can marry a man with more money?"

She returned his look with one of such sheer incredulity, followed by such flaming anger, that he was abashed.

"Randi, I didn't mean —"

He had steered her almost into the DANGER sign under the scaffolding, and now he drew her away. For a moment Randi stood looking at the activity about the building, trying to regain her control. This was the last time she would see Willis, except remotely and casually, as people are bound to encounter each other from time to time in a village. She did not want this final meeting to end in anger and bitterness that would leave a sting behind them. She must find something safe, something neutral to talk about.

"I never realized until this morning," she said, "how dangerous this work can be. Mrs. Echo told me her husband nearly fell yesterday because the ropes holding the scaffolding slipped. I love watching things being built, don't you? I always stop here, morning and evening, to look on for a while."

By this time they had reached the corner where Willis had to turn off for his office.

"I suppose you are still working for Old Money-bags?" he said lightly.

"Mr. King?" She made the correction without stressing the criticism of his manners that underlay it. "Yes. By the way, how did you learn about the job, Willis?"

He shrugged. "You know how things get around, and Old Moneybags is always news. I thought you might as well get that dough as some strange gal from the city."

She held out her hand. "Thank you for suggesting it, Willis. This is good-by and good luck."

He took her hand, tossed back the long lock of hair that had fallen into his eyes, gave her his boyish, confident smile. "All roads lead to Rome," he said, "so I'll be seeing you soon, sweet."

Her brown eyes were very direct. There was no smile on her lips. "What does that mean?"

"There are lots of ways of accomplishing the same end," he told her and he, too, was not smiling. "Perhaps, after all, this might be for the best."

ii

That morning there was no car in the driveway and no distress in Luther's face when he opened the door.

"Good morning, Miss Scott." He beamed at her. "Isn't it a beautiful day? Pity to be indoors. I can't remember our ever having such a spring." He dropped his voice. "That nurse! One of the maids heard her complaining to the housekeeper that she ought to move down from the third floor and have one of those lovely suites on the second floor. To be nearer her patient in case he needed her!" He rolled his eyes expressively. "Any time! Give that woman an inch — well, some day Mr. King will be fed up with her, trying to make a permanent place for herself in this house. And good riddance to bad rubbish, I say. Did you notice he made short work of getting rid of her at lunch time yesterday? I almost laughed out loud."

As Randi was careful about gossiping, he shifted the subject. "You are to go right up. Mr. King is expecting you."

Feeling somewhat self-conscious after yesterday's interview, Randi went into the library where Jonas King was waiting for her. This morning he was not seated at his desk as usual but standing at a window looking out on the spacious grounds and the charming little guesthouse, built like a Swiss chalet, beyond the rose garden.

He turned around, smiling, but except that he called her Randi instead of Miss Scott, as he had done until the day before, there was no change in his manner. When he had said that her decision would make no difference to her job he had meant it.

Not until she was seated beside his desk, notebook in hand, pencils laid out neatly on the desk beside her, did she become aware, sunk as she was in her own thoughts, in her memory of her meeting — and final parting — with Willis, that Mr. King was not, as usual, going over his notes, phrasing in his mind the opening sentence of his dictation. He was watching her face.

"Something has happened, Randi, hasn't it?"

She nodded.

"Something bad?"

She considered for a moment. "I don't really know," she said honestly. "Something upsetting, pretty shattering, as a matter of fact, but — after all, I suppose it was for the best. You can't live with a lie, can you?"

He smiled wryly. "Some people seem to be able to do so without difficulty."

"Well, I couldn't."

He smiled again. "I know. That's why I made that — suggestion of mine yesterday. It's a pleasant thing to know that one is surrounded by people one can trust completely." He saw her expression and shook his head. "No, I'm not going to repeat the proposal that so distressed you. Shall we try to dismiss it from our minds entirely?"

"I'll never forget how proud I am that you asked me," she told him simply. "How grateful."

"No, no! I don't want your gratitude. It's too much of a burden for anyone to bear." He leaned forward, studying her more keenly. "If we put all that to one side, is there any way, any way at all, I can be of service to you in dealing with this — shattering thing that has happened?"

"Thank you." Randi's clear brown eyes met his candidly. "But I'm the only one who can deal with it. You see, I'm not engaged any more. It has gone on so long that I feel — sort of — lost. That's all."

He smiled at her understatement but he was proud of her. "That's natural enough and I'm not going to tell you that these things pass, that you'll get over it, even though —"

There was an answering smile in her eyes now. "Even though they do pass. You are right, of course. I feel hurt and stunned and — cheated, somehow, because nothing of what I thought about Willis and his feeling for me was true. But I'm not heartbroken. I'd be a hypocrite to say I am."

Jonas laughed outright. "There speaks an honest girl who won't lie, even to herself, about her own feelings. More power to you!"

She opened her notebook and reached for a pencil, feeling that too much time had already been devoted to her personal affairs, but he shook his head.

"Not yet, Randi. There's plenty of time for the book. What went wrong with that engagement?"

She fought a battle with her pride and then told him the truth. "I went to meet him last evening; we always have, or rather had, dates on Wednesdays and Saturdays. I found him with another girl, kissing her in a way — there could be no mistake. He never felt like that about me. So I — just went home and didn't answer the telephone when he called."

"Surely he won't let you go that easily! No man would."

Randi flushed a little at his tone. "Oh, he didn't. When I left the house this morning he was waiting for me. He said — she was just a grateful client. He said — I wanted an excuse to break our engagement because I would rather have money and a big — house —" Her voice trailed off.

"Well, you and I know better, don't we? And this young man, if he has any sense at all, knows better too. Did he just leave it at that?"

"He said," Randi was frowning, trying to understand that curious change in Willis's attitude, "that all roads lead to Rome; that perhaps this was the best way, after all."

There was sharp speculation in the look he gave her. "What did you tell me is the name of this rather idiotic young man?"

"Willis Jameson."

He repeated it to himself, shook his head. "For a moment I thought — but, no, I don't know anyone of that name."

"Mr. King," Randi asked, leaning forward, "how many people knew that you wanted to hire a secretary, that you were planning to write a book and that the position would be open?"

Whatever he had expected it was not that question. He looked at her in astonishment. Then his cool gray eyes narrowed in thought. "How *did* you learn about the job?" he countered. "I hadn't got around to advertising or applying to an employment agency."

She moistened her lips. "Willis told me. He said I might as well apply because it would pay a lot more than I was earning."

He nodded thoughtfully. "On one of the few occasions when Hubert has honored me with a visit, I told him I didn't like rusting out; I had to have some sort of occupation to keep my mind alert. I would like to write a book and, in that case, I would need someone to take dictation, do typing; someone intelligent enough to handle occasional research, check data, all that."

"Your brother?" Randi frowned and shook her head. "I don't see —"

"What association there can be between my brother and your former fiancé? Neither do I." Jonas drew his notes toward him, pushed them away again. He spoke abruptly. "Randi, circumstances have altered rather drastically with you since yesterday. I told you then that my offer stands. . . . It still does."

She sat staring at her small hands, thinking of her break with Willis, remembering Melody coughing in the night and trying to smother the sound so as not to disturb her sister. A marriage of mutual convenience. She would have to say farewell to love, but in a way that had already been done. Instead, she would have friendship and mutual respect and trust. She would know unswerving kindness. Melody would be safe and so would Jonas King; at least he would be safe from his brother's attempts to injure him.

Compared with the lot of the majority of women hers would be a wonderful and rewarding life. And it would not be all one-sided acceptance of kindness either. She could bring sunlight into this wonderful but dark house, drive away some of its shadows.

Without a word she held out her hand. Jonas took it in his, looked deep into her eyes, smiled, and then bent over to kiss her fingers.

V

JONAS set down the telephone, smiling. "I just talked with my lawyer. Everything is clear and he will arrange matters for us. This afternoon my doctor is coming to give us our blood tests."

"This afternoon!" Randi was breathless with the speed at which things were happening.

"Then, according to Connecticut law, in four days we can take out the license and be married immediately." Jonas shoved away the notes for his book impatiently. "There is such a lot to be done, so many arrangements to make." Color had risen in his cheeks, and his eyes were bright. He seemed to have taken on a new lease of life. "My lawyer will be here some time tomorrow to discuss my new will. I've already outlined the provisions over the telephone."

For a moment the walls seemed to be closing in on Randi. What had she done? When she had made that impulsive gesture she had not dreamed of the swiftness with which Mr. King — Jonas, she corrected herself; from now on she must call him Jonas, this man who could easily be her father — would set things moving.

"I think," he went on, "that a wedding should be more than a mere civil ceremony. If the idea pleases you I would like to be married here in the house by my clergyman. You will want your sister to be present, of course, and I'll ask Cary to be my attendant. But I do not intend to invite my brother. I don't want to see him here until it is all over. Signed, sealed, and delivered. I don't want him to get any ideas." The smile was gone and his face looked grim.

"But surely you can't believe that he would attempt to interfere," Randi exclaimed in horror.

"Let's say that I intend to take every possible precaution to insure my own safety until after I have married you and signed my new will, and the Foundation is all set up. Until then I'll give strict instructions that my brother is not to be admitted to this house. After that — well, a man can't live permanently in a state of siege. Anyhow, when Hubert realizes that there is nothing for him to gain, he will probably drop all these ugly attempts of his to shock me into a heart attack."

He broke off as Luther came in, rolling the table he had brought up on the elevator, moving it between Randi and Jonas, removing silver covers.

"Will that be all, sir?"

"Yes. Oh, just a moment, Luther. I wish you would inform the staff that Miss Scott has consented to become my wife. We will be married within the week. I shall expect her to receive the same excellent service they have given me. This afternoon, I would like the housekeeper to show her over the whole house, so that she can decide what rooms she wants for herself and what changes she may care to have made."

Surprised as he must have been by the announcement, Luther, as a well-trained servant, betrayed no inkling of it. "On behalf of the entire household, sir, may I offer our heartiest congratulations?"

"Thank you, Luther." Jonas smiled at Randi, who said, "Thank you."

"When would you like the housekeeper to report?"

Randi looked at Jonas, who said, smiling, "I think we will put the book aside for the present. Your time is your own, my dear."

"After lunch then, Luther," Randi said.

While they were eating lunch Jonas said, "There are a number of arrangements to make. First, of course, you must have an adequate wardrobe. There will be a certain amount of entertaining for you to do, especially in the early days as a bride. And you must, of course, have a ring." He frowned. "Sometimes it is trying to be physically so inadequate. I'm afraid I can't make the trip to New York. I suppose I could have the jeweler send a man out. But why doesn't Cary deputize for me and select your engagement and wedding rings and a gift for the bride? You might, at the same time, get whatever clothes you will need for the wedding and the next few weeks. Later, of course, you can do your shopping at leisure."

"I feel," Randi confessed, "that I am being a great expense to you."

Jonas laughed. "I don't think you need worry about that."

When Luther had removed the table, the house-keeper, Mrs. Wilkes, arrived to take Randi on a tour of the house. Randi had never encountered her before, and they exchanged looks of veiled but equal curiosity. For each of them the support of the other would be invaluable and smooth the way in the future.

Mrs. Wilkes resembled a governess rather than a housekeeper, a tall, slim, trim woman of middle age with iron-gray hair, simply arranged, and an unexpectedly smart black dress. In her eyes Randi read an expression which told her that Mrs. Wilkes was taken aback by her youth and suspected her of being a gold digger.

Together they went through the big house, while Mrs. Wilkes displayed the drawing room, a less formal living room, and the big dining room and smaller breakfast parlor. At the back were the kitchen, butler's pantry, and a servants' living room, and above, the servants' bedrooms.

It was all finely furnished, revealed excellent taste, but nonetheless the general effect was one of heaviness, of gloom, of weight, of darkness.

The second floor consisted of the great library and Jonas's private suite on the right side of the big hall-way. On the left there were two smaller suites, each consisting of sitting room, bedroom, and bath, while the third floor was made up of single bedrooms, each with bath. There were, at the time, only four servants who lived in the house, Mrs. Wilkes explained: the butler and his wife who was the cook, Mr. King's valet, and herself. Two maids came in by the day, as did the men who took care of the grounds, and cleaning women and laundresses.

After a little hesitation Randi selected for her own use the suite at the back of the second floor, chiefly because the one on the front looked out up the wide sweep of lawn studded by trees and ending at the great wall which enclosed the estate and gave her a breathless feeling of being shut in. The rooms at the back had a lovely open view of gardens, of bushes just beginning to turn green, of distant trees, and the charming little Swiss chalet that served as a guesthouse.

The extent of the house, its luxurious appointments, the size of the staff, all impressed Randi, but again with that feeling of weight. She had not realized what kind of position would be occupied by Mrs. Jonas King. She wondered whether she would be able to carry out her task as a hostess adequately, to plan the social activities that would be expected of her, to organize the machinery of this establishment.

"I do hope, Mrs. Wilkes," she said impulsively, "that you will be patient with me. I have so much to learn and I am going to depend greatly on you for assistance and advice."

She could have said nothing more calculated to please the housekeeper, who had been monarch of this domain for fifteen years and feared that her authority would be challenged if not undermined by this young woman whom she could not help regarding as an interloper.

"It will be a pleasure, Miss Scott," she replied. "The staff, as you must know, is devoted to Mr. King. It will be a pleasure to have you as mistress of this house."

When Randi returned to the library, Jonas looked up to smile at her.

"What is the verdict?" he asked.

"It's a wonderful house," Randi said warmly.

"I'm glad you like it." Jonas looked quizzically over his glasses at the handsome nurse who was preparing his medicine. "Miss Scott," he said, "has been inspecting her new domain. She has honored me by consenting to become my wife."

Mavis started, splashing water on the desk. She leaned over hastily to wipe it up. "You are to be congratulated, Miss Scott," she said, her voice cold, her eyes hot with anger. "You are a very clever woman."

"I think," Jonas said, "that I should be the one to be congratulated."

"Do you?" In her rage Mavis had lost all control, all judgment. She went swiftly to the door, turned back. "Do you indeed, Mr. King."

ii

"That settles it," Jonas said. "Miss Bertram will have to go. In any case, I haven't really needed the services of a nurse for weeks; her presence here has been more or less a precautionary measure. My valet can do all that I need."

He looked younger and happier than Randi had yet seen him. "There's another thing, Randi. Will you go out to the guesthouse and ask Cary Hamilton if he can give me a few minutes? I'd like to get things settled and arrange to have him take you into New York tomorrow. Do you mind?"

He looked so eager that Randi said quickly, "Of course not." She had left her lined raincoat in a cloakroom off the main hall on the first floor, and she put it on, though the sun was so warm that she hardly needed it.

She let herself out and walked around the house, following a garden path to the guesthouse. Never before had she had an opportunity to inspect the grounds so closely; Jonas had been fortunate in finding skilled landscape gardeners; the flower beds were beautifully laid out, but wherever possible the natural wildness of the terrain had been allowed to have its own way. A little rustic bridge crossed a stream whose banks had not been tampered with, and the sun made stars dance on the rippling water.

Randi stood looking down at the happy-sounding brook and thought how Melody would love this place. She had not as yet mentioned bringing Melody here to live, but she was sure that Jonas would concur with her wishes. And when another winter came her sister could go to the Southwest and be safe from the rigors of the harsh New England season.

Randi was startled out of her preoccupation with her own thoughts by a voice saying, "Hello!"

She looked down to see a small boy staring at her.

Crisp blond curls, big blue eyes, cheeks like red flames.
He was about four.

"Hello yourself," she replied.

He looked back and then crouched down beside a
bush so that he would be out of sight of the guesthouse,
and Randi suspected that he had escaped from the
powers that be and he was in hiding.

"The ground's damp," she told him. "You ought to
have a coat."

"I won't. I won't either have a coat. I don't want a
coat. I'm a big boy now." He was standing beside her,
his fists clenched, head flung back in defiance.

"You don't act like a big boy, just like a silly small
one," Randi said, repressing her desire to pick him up
in her arms.

"I'm not either silly."

"Well, you don't need to yell at me. I can hear you."
Randi went past him toward the chalet.

"Hey!" protested the little boy, who was not accustomed to being ignored. He ran to catch up with her
and gave her an enchanting smile, calculated to disarm
a heart of ice. "I'm not silly."

The door opened and John Lancing called, "Andy!
Oh, there you are. I've told you not to go out without
your coat." He saw Randi and his face lighted up.
"Miss Scott! This is pleasant. Come in." He gave a
harassed look around him. "I'm afraid this room is a
mess."

That, Randi thought, was an understatement. Andy

had been playing with a train and she had to watch her step not to fall over the tracks that were spread out on the carpet. A discarded toy engine lay on a couch. A picture book with torn covers had been left on a chair.

As he picked up the abandoned toys Lancing apologized. "Things aren't always in such bad shape. Well, I'm trying to cope but without much success. Poor Cary will wish he had never asked us. He has had to retreat to his own room upstairs in order to work in peace. If I could just find someone who could make this youngster of mine a full-time job, I'd feel like a new man. As it is I'm beginning to feel very old."

Randi laughed. "You know, Mr. Lancing, I was telling my sister about your son last evening. She loves children and she has a magic touch with them. They always obey her, but she doesn't curb their individuality or anything like that. The neighborhood children adore her. She could do so much for Andy."

His face brightened. "You mean it? Where can I find this paragon?"

Randi laughed at his eagerness.

"No," he insisted, "I really want to find her. In fact, I'd like to talk to her today if you think she would be interested."

"I'm sure she would be. We talked about establishing a school for prekindergarten children, but it's more satisfactory and rewarding, of course, to devote all one's time to a single child."

"The drawback," Lancing admitted, "to being the only child involved is that Andy might become awfully attached to her and this would have to be just a temporary arrangement. I'm on leave of absence for six months. But my work is in Arizona and I'll have to go back in the fall. It would be a pity to have Andy grow too fond of someone and then break off the relationship."

"Of course," Randi said, her eyes shining, "if it worked out at all, that would be a perfect solution for Melody because she needs a warm, dry climate."

"Melody? What a lovely name."

"She's a lovely person," Randi told him huskily.

While John Lancing was taking the address and asking how to find the house, Cary Hamilton came down the stairs. The main floor of the guesthouse consisted of a large living room and a small kitchenette. The second floor had three bedrooms, one of them very small, and only one bath.

"I thought I heard — why, Miss Scott!" Again she felt that extraordinary sensation when his hand clasped hers, felt that curious sense of recognition, almost of belonging, when their eyes met. It was absurd. She didn't know the man and yet she felt that she had known him always.

Something in her mind said, "Too late! Too late!" As though she were guilty of an act of disloyalty she brushed it aside. She had determined the course of her life by her own free will. There could be no turning back now.

"Mr. King would be very grateful if you could go over to see him, Mr. Hamilton," she said. "He said he wouldn't keep you long but he wants to ask a favor of you."

"He couldn't ask anything I wouldn't be glad to do for him," Cary replied. "He is one of the finest men I know. Are you coming with me?"

Randi hesitated. It would be better if Cary were to hear Jonas's announcement when she was not there. She did not ask herself why she did not want to be present when he learned of her imminent marriage.

"Stay and play with me," Andy said peremptorily. "I like you."

She laughed. "I'll be over later," she said.

VI

CARY walked swiftly through the grounds, over the rustic bridge, and toward the house. Miss Scott. He didn't even know her first name. He didn't know anything except that he had taken one look at her and found what he had been seeking all his life. He whistled softly to himself as he went up the steps and rang the bell. What a spring! What a glorious spring! And suppose, by the time summer came, the girl were to learn to feel as he did. He was exultant. He felt invulnerable, as though he could tackle the world single-handed.

"Afternoon, Luther," he said, and at the butler's gesture he ran lightly up the stairs.

"Come in, Cary. Nice of you to come so quickly."

"Your Miss Scott said you wanted to ask me something."

Jonas smiled. "In a way that is the gist of what I have to say." Seeing the puzzled expression on Cary's face, he explained, "*My* Miss Scott. Randi Scott has just promised to marry me."

Cary, who had been about to fill his pipe, stood arrested. He drew a long breath and at last expelled it in a sigh. "Oh," he said. He added with difficulty, "I am glad for you. She is — very lovely."

Part of his mind was saying, "Randi. Jonas King's Randi. Promised to marry him. He's too old for her. He's an invalid. So why?" And an insidious voice he could not ignore, said, "He's a very rich man. It must be the money."

At Jonas's gesture he sat down, his face as expressionless as he could make it, but the two men had known each other for a long time. Cary had an uncomfortable feeling that Jonas King had read his thoughts with a fair degree of accuracy.

"We're going to be married just as soon as the law allows."

"Marry in haste." Cary tried to sound as though he were joking.

"And repent at leisure? No, I don't think so, in this case. There is a reason for the haste. Of course this isn't a love match. Don't misunderstand."

"I don't." Cary's voice was dry but not, he hoped, as bitter as he felt. "It's natural, after all, for a girl to marry for her security."

"Not hers. It is my security that is involved. One of these days I'll tell you about it. After all, you are going to be vitally concerned."

"Concerned in what?" Cary's tone was startled. Did Jonas King suspect his feeling for Randi?

"I'm not able to get around as much as I should like to," Jonas said in his quiet voice. "What I would greatly appreciate would be having you take Randi to New York tomorrow. I want you to pick out the engagement and wedding rings and a gift for the bride. I thought of a diamond bracelet, but use your own judgment, and consult her taste, of course. She'll have to get a few clothes for the wedding, too. Will you look after her for me, Cary?"

"I'll look after her, sir," Cary assured him, and his voice was flat. "For you."

"I'm relying on you. She may need to call on you for help or advice now and then."

"It strikes me that she is quite capable of looking after herself." Cary could not keep the bitterness out of his voice.

Jonas studied the younger man's face. "You are mistaken," he said quietly. "Randi has all the vulnerability that comes of being too trusting. She has the weakness that comes of being more eager to help others than to protect herself. I am not a fool, Cary, whatever you may be thinking at the moment. I have not been trapped into marriage by a pretty face and an ambitious, unscrupulous girl. Perhaps it is too much to ask you at this point to trust my judgment. But I do ask you to keep an open mind. Now then, let's get down to details. I'll call Tiffany's where I have an account. What I would prefer —"

He talked and Cary, graven-faced, jotted down notes. When Jonas had finished with his suggestions he said casually, "It occurs to me that it might be pleasant for Randi to have a little festivity in connection with her approaching wedding. Why don't you get theater tickets and take her to dinner? Perhaps dance later. I keep an apartment at the Plaza where she can stay for the night. You could put up at your club and drive her back in the morning. All right?"

"All right," Cary agreed. "That sounds like a pleasant program." But his mind rebelled. He did not intend to spend an evening alone with Randi Scott. The girl whom he had discovered by a miracle was going to marry another man; worse than that, it was the man to whom he owed the most, the man whom he most respected. He could not, in loyalty, even raise a hand to prevent the marriage and to plead his own cause.

The only peace he could attain would be to stay as far away from her as possible. He would bring her home as soon as her errands were finished tomorrow, and in a few days he would find some plausible reason why he would have to leave the guesthouse. He remembered Jonas saying he wanted him to put down roots, to regard the place as his home. Well, it was one place he'd try hard never to see again.

The exultant feeling with which he had entered the house was gone. He would never again find anyone like Randi. Too late! Too late! It would have been better if he had never known of her existence, if he had gone on seeking for the girl who would be like his dreams. At least then he would not have this sense of aching loss.

When he got back to the guesthouse he found Lancing and Randi sitting on the floor with the little boy, all three playing with the train. Randi's cheeks were flushed from exertion and she looked prettier than ever. She gave him a quick, almost shy glance.

"I understand, Miss Scott, that you are going to marry Jonas King." Cary's voice was unexpectedly formal, aloof. "You are making him a very happy man."

"I'm — glad," she said lamely. Her eyes met his, held, and then moved quickly away. She got to her feet. "I must get back."

"Don't go!" Andy ordered her.

"I must."

"No! If you go I'll yell."

"You go right ahead," Randi said. "But then I won't come back at all. I don't like playing with noisy people."

His mouth opened, he glared at her, and then his face lighted. "All right. I'm good now," he assured her.

Again Randi resisted the impulse to hug him. "Fine!" She promised, "We'll play together some other time."

"Are you sure it's all right for me to call on your sister?" John Lancing asked. "If she has the same sure hand with children that you have —"

"She's twice as good," Randi assured him. "She should have a dozen of her own."

When she had gone back to the big stone house, Lancing said, "What was that, Cary? Is it true that Miss Scott is going to marry Mr. King?"

Cary nodded. "He wants me to take her to New York tomorrow to buy a ring and see that she has a chance to select her wedding clothes. He also suggested that I take her out for the evening."

"A kind of deputy bridegroom," John laughed, and then he saw his friend's face, saw the spasm of pain that had crossed it before Cary could regain control. Lancing's lips puckered in a soundless whistle. He had known Cary for a long time, known him increasingly well since their interests had become the same. There was no man for whom he had a higher regard. His wife Helen had said he was the most attractive man she had ever met, and she had repeatedly introduced him to pretty girls, most of whom made it clear that they too found him attractive. But Cary, who had appeared to be invulnerable to the charms of the girls who had thrown themselves upon his notice, had fallen for the girl his friend was going to marry. He was taking it hard, still rocking from the blow. John, observing the drawn expression on his face, sought words of consolation and could find none.

"Miss Scott tells me her sister would be wonderful at taking care of Andy," he said, speaking as lightly as he could. "Why don't you come along while I talk to her?" He did not want to leave Cary alone with his thoughts. "It's much too nice a day to be indoors and a walk may help work off some of this little monster's superfluous energy."

"All right," Cary agreed dully. In any case he was in no mood to go back to work.

The two young men set off, regulating their longer stride to the short steps of the small boy who laughed and chattered and bounced along between them. When they reached the spot on Main Street where the new building was being erected they had to drag him away by force. Andy wanted to stay and watch. When his father finally picked him up in his arms he screamed with rage.

Lancing looked in perplexity at Cary, wondering how to cope with this sort of thing, and Andy, with the intuitive awareness of even quite young children, realized that he had the whip hand. He continued to scream.

The little cottage where Randi and Melody lived was on a small corner lot. There was a neat hedge, a small lawn, and a minuscule flower bed in which a girl, kneeling on a cushion, was loosening the soil around a rosebush. Soft light hair like a bright silken cloud hung over her shoulders.

At the sound of the little boy's howls she turned around, her eyes on his flushed face, aware of his thwarted anger, his determination to have his own way. This must be the little cherub Randi had mentioned to her. She was so absorbed in the child that she was not conscious of the two young men who stood looking at her, at the exquisite face with its dark-fringed eyes.

How lovely she is, Lancing thought. Like Helen in a way, but Helen was never so beautiful. . . . It was not disloyalty to his dead wife. The feeling was rather a projection of his love for her, a tracing of a resemblance, a welcoming of it. At the same time he was aware that this was a rarer beauty than he had ever encountered before.

She isn't like Randi, Cary thought in relief. Not at all like Randi. . . . Randi was sunlight; this girl like the softer light of the moon. They were both lovely, but he was glad they were different. At the moment he knew that he must get back all his control and steel

himself in detachment before he saw Randi again. For
Jonas's sake and for his own honor, he must not let her
suspect that he loved her.

"Well!" Melody said in a shocked voice. She did not
appear to be cowed by the tantrum or impressed by it.

The howls of rage stopped. Andy wriggled in his
father's arms. "Down! Let me down!" he ordered in
his imperious way. When his father set him on his feet
he went straight to Melody and for a long moment the
two stared at each other gravely. Then he squatted
down beside her. "Let me help! I can dig too."

A couple of hours later Lancing said authoritatively,
"That's enough, Andy."

"No!"

"You are going to tire Miss Melody if you keep that
up."

"I won't tire her. I like her," Andy assured both his
father and Melody.

"We all like her," Lancing said in a tone that made
Cary look at him quickly, "but we don't want her to be
so tired she won't want to play with you again. So if
you want her to let us come back —"

"I'll go home now," Andy agreed readily. He came
close to pat Melody's cheek, to look anxiously into her
face, seeking her approval. She took him in her arms,
her cheek against the soft blond curls. He hugged her
strenuously.

"Can I come back tomorrow?" he asked, and his
father grinned as he perceived that the child had, in a
short period of time, found it wiser to ask than to
demand.

"Are you sure you can put up with him, Miss Melody?"

"Of course," she declared, her lovely blue eyes shining with pleasure. "Andy and I are going to be partners. There are a lot of things I need help with around here."

"I can dig," he reminded her eagerly.

"You certainly can. Like a puppy burying a bone."

"I am not," he began, and then burst into delighted laughter. "A puppy with a bone! I am not! And you'll tell me another story?"

Melody pretended to consider the matter. "I think I could do that."

Lancing took her hand. "I can't tell you how grateful I am, Miss Melody. Andy needs —" He stopped when he saw her expression. A few minutes earlier, when Andy had been running happily around with the Brooks children from next door, she had said, "Please don't talk about him in his hearing. It will only make him self-conscious and children understand so much more than we think. He'll be all right. He needs discipline and love he can depend on, and more than anything else he needs other children to cut him down to size." And she gave a mischievous laugh.

Once more they shook hands gravely and then she turned to Cary.

"I've been wondering — aren't you the Mr. Hamilton who has been fighting our local Fascists?"

"Local or national. Wherever I find them," he told her.

"I've been so interested in following the work you

have been doing. I wonder Randi didn't tell me that
you are staying with Mr. King. You are one of her
heroes."

"I expect she had other, more interesting, things to
talk about," Cary said.

At something in his voice Melody gave him a startled
look.

The two men started home, with Andy prancing
between them, chattering about Melody and the games
they would play tomorrow, about the story she had told
him, and the Brooks children.

"She'll be wonderful for Andy," Lancing said as the
little boy ran ahead.

Cary grinned at him. "She'll be wonderful for you,
too, or else I miss my guess."

"I think she's the loveliest human being I ever saw,"
Lancing said soberly. They walked on in silence. "You
know, I got the odd impression that she doesn't know
her younger sister is going to marry Mr. King."

"Probably she doesn't. They just became engaged
this morning, as I understand it," Cary told him.

Lancing started to speak, broke off to shout, "Andy!
Come back here. Keep away from that building." He
ran to catch hold of the boy and draw him back from
under the swing stage.

Andy looked up in fascination. "Look, Daddy!
There's someone with a knife!"

But Lancing and Cary were not looking up; they
were staring appalled at the girl with her shining cap of
black hair, who was so deep in thought that she did not

notice the DANGER sign had been moved, she did not observe the sudden sagging of the platform.

The alarmed yell of the man on the platform was echoed by a shout of horror as Cary leaped forward, seized Randi, rushed her out into the street. One end of the stage tipped, fell with a crash to the sidewalk. Up above, a white-faced man clung to the one sound rope, dangling in mid-air.

At the sound of the crash, workmen began swarming away from the building, people were coming out of the department store, the bank, the drugstore, gathering to stare.

Cary picked up the swaying Randi, who was too shocked to grasp what had happened, and carried her back onto the sidewalk, well away from the building. For once Andy was completely silent, too absorbed in what was going on to make a sound.

Cary's arms tightened around Randi, holding her against him. For a moment his lips brushed over her hair. Then he set her on her feet, his hands on her arms to steady her.

"Are you all right?" His voice was hoarse with strain.

"I — I guess you saved my life." She looked at the fallen platform, which had crashed on the spot where she had stood only seconds before.

"Oh, Randi," Cary groaned. His hands tighted on her arms. Then, with an effort of will, he released her.

The workman who had been hanging onto the rope slid cautiously downward onto the sidewalk and stood mopping his head. Randi noticed that he had a black eye and realized that this must be Mr. Echo, whose pronouncements were relayed to her day after day.

"I thought I was a goner," he admitted. "If we had been working higher up — I don't see how it could have happened. Second time that rope's slipped. The second time. And the lady — she shouldn't have been right under us. She could have been killed. That's why we keep that DANGER sign there. Now that's funny. Someone moved the sign."

"Just a minute." Cary, moving cautiously, worked his way slowly up the slanting platform, looked at the severed rope at the second-floor level. After a long time he called down, his voice hoarse, "My God, the rope *was* cut!"

VII

$\mathcal{A}$T Randi's insistence the two men left her before she reached the cottage. She didn't, she explained, want to upset Melody by having to be escorted home.

The precaution failed to work. After one look, Melody cried out, "Randi! What's happened? You're as white as a sheet."

Striving to speak as calmly as possible and to underplay the accident, Randi told her about the severing of the rope and how the platform had crashed on the spot where she was standing.

"You might have been killed!" Melody cried.

"Well, I wasn't. Just a bit shaken. It was really all over before I even realized what was happening."

"And the man on the scaffolding wasn't hurt either?"

"Scared out of his wits. That's all. I don't blame him for that. And, by the way, I think he must be Mrs. Echo's husband. She was telling me this morning there was some sort of near accident yesterday because of that scaffolding and he got a black eye. This one certainly had."

"How on earth could a thing like that happen? How

could anyone be so careless when human life was at stake?"

"According to little Andy, there was someone up there with a knife, and when Mr. Hamilton investigated he said the rope had been cut."

While the two girls were eating dinner, Melody said, "Do you think it's possible, Randi, that someone deliberately tried to hurt Mrs. Echo's husband?"

"Mrs. Echo's husband! That sounds ridiculous. And I can't imagine why anyone should have any resentment against him. Such a harmless little man he appeared to be. But of course, the fact that the rope was deliberately cut so that the staging would fall — that much is true."

"How on earth did you happen to be right under it when it fell? I thought the sidewalk was always blocked off so pedestrians wouldn't be injured by something falling."

"That's a queer thing, too. Someone had moved away the DANGER sign, and you know how people are. We don't look up as a rule unless something attracts our attention. If it hadn't been for Cary —"

"As long as I live I'll remember what we both owe him for that," Melody said fervently. "I told him this afternoon he had always been a hero of yours, and now he proves it. Why on earth didn't you tell me that he was a guest of Mr. King's? We've both admired his work so much. And he is absolutely charming."

Randi changed the subject abruptly. "How did you get along with little Andy? He looks like a cherub, but I'm afraid he is really a spoiled little brat."

"He's a darling," Melody said warmly. "All that's wrong with him is that people have been giving in to him, letting him have or do whatever he demanded because he is so charming, and now he is deliberately exploiting his charm. When that doesn't work he howls for what he wants. I can cure him of that in a few weeks at the outside. You just watch and see."

"Then you are planning to take him on. He won't be too strenuous for you?"

"Of course he won't. Oh Randi, if you knew what it will mean for me to be independent!"

"But you won't need to work now," Randi told her. "There is going to be plenty of money for both of us."

"Your salary." Melody shook her head. "No, I want to be on my own. And if things work out, that is, if Andy and I get along as I think we are bound to do, Mr. Lancing may suggest that I go on looking after the boy when he returns to Arizona. That is where he lives permanently. Wouldn't that be wonderful, Randi? You won't have to bother with me."

"Bother! How can you say that?"

"I want you free to live your own life," Melody said firmly.

Randi got up to clear the table and stack the dishes. It seemed to take her longer than usual. When she came back she said abruptly, while her courage was high, "Melody, I changed my mind this morning. Willis is out of my life forever, so I — I told Jonas King that I would marry him."

"Oh Randi, no!" It was a cry of protest, of anguish. "No, you mustn't. This is something you are doing on the rebound because of Willis. You can't marry a man you don't love. It isn't fair to him any more than it is to you. You simply can't." She sounded frantic and Randi summoned up a smile, trying to quiet her, to reassure her.

"It's all right," she said gaily. "It's going to be wonderful. If you could only see how happy he is about it, how eager and interested and alive. We're going to be married within a week."

"Oh, no!" Melody sobbed. "You are ruining your life out of an impulse."

"You don't know him, Melody. Wait until you meet him before you make up your mind about him."

Melody dried her eyes and looked directly at her sister. "Randi, you are capable of making any sacrifice. Who should know that better than I? But if you are doing this for me, I implore you to reconsider. In the first place, Mr. Lancing is going to have me take care of Andy so I won't need your financial help. In the second place, there is just no excuse for a marriage without love."

Randi made no comment.

"It can't be the money, can it, Randi?" Melody tried again. "For yourself, I mean. You're the least grasping — that is, it seems so impossible — I can't believe you'd be influenced by the money."

"No, of course it isn't for the money," Randi assured her.

"But are you doing it with the idea that you can give me better care?"

"When he first asked me," Randi said slowly, "I couldn't help thinking what a difference it might make to you. You could live in a place where you would be healthy and completely independent of me. It was Jonas, by the way, who pointed out that it wasn't good for you to have me sort of smothering you with anxiety and care. He's a very understanding and wise man, Melody."

"But now that I shall be able to take care of myself, why are you planning to go ahead with this impossible marriage? And in such a hurry?"

"Because," Randi said at last, realizing that only the truth would satisfy her sister, "it might — it just might possibly save Jonas's life, or at least prolong it." Groping for words, she went on to explain the danger in which Jonas King stood.

"You mean that Hubert King is back of that All-American Party attempt to propagandize schoolchildren?" Melody exclaimed in horror.

"He is one of them. Without money he can't hope to have as much influence as he would like. So you see why he must not be allowed to have the money. By marrying me and drawing up a new will, Jonas can make it almost impossible for Hubert to make any claims for inheritance, and, at the same time, to make sure his money will be properly used."

"But do you mean to tell me," Melody was incredulous, "that he is going to trust you, almost a complete stranger, with the handling of his whole fortune? Why, he must be worth millions!"

"Oh, no! He'll just leave me an adequate income — I don't know how much — but the bulk of his property and his house are to go to a foundation."

"And Mr. Hamilton, of course, will carry on the fight against those horrible and dangerous people. Well, I begin to understand how you feel about it but I still think you should let someone else handle it."

"Melody! You don't really mean that. This is our war, yours and mine, as well as that of the rest of the people of this country. I don't expect to ask someone else to do my fighting, but I wouldn't have much respect for myself if I didn't do my share."

Melody held out her hand. "You're right," she said simply. "I keep thinking — where you are concerned — that what matters most is making you happy. But other things count too."

The doorbell rang and Randi went to answer it. She stared in disbelief.

"Hello, Willis." She stood blocking the doorway, watching him without moving. "I think we have already said good-by."

"Randi!" He caught her in his arms, holding her almost fiercely.

She was aware, in some surprise, that he was shaking, that his face was ashen. She released herself more gently than she meant to. "What on earth is wrong, Willis? I didn't expect to see you here again."

"I just heard about the — accident. You were nearly killed. Oh, my God, Randi! If anything had happened to you —"

Never, in the three years she had known him, in the

two years they had been engaged to be married, had Randi heard his voice like this, throbbing with genuine feeling. He was not only shocked by her near-accident; he was horrified. He was, she realized, looking at his drained face, which suddenly was no longer boyish, which was almost old, afraid.

And then she knew and for a moment her veins seemed to be filled with ice. Their conversation of that morning appeared in a new light, fell into place. He had known of Jonas King's proposal the day before; he had assumed that she had accepted him. Could it be that Willis was responsible, at least to some degree, for the accident? *Someone* wanted to prevent her from marrying Jonas. It was not solely Jonas King who was in danger; it was Randi Scott as well.

She steadied herself against the open door, her thoughts whirling. In all her twenty-two years she had never before encountered active evil. She was not frightened for herself but she was sick with horror.

"Willis," she asked, her voice so low it was almost a whisper, "whom did you tell that I always stop when I pass that new building to watch the construction, and the times at which I pass there?"

"Randi!" he cried in protest.

Behind her, Melody echoed with a gasp, "Randi!"

"I — what do you mean?" Willis was taken aback, rocked off balance by her sudden attack; he was attempting to bluster.

"How well do you know Hubert King?" Her mind had made the inevitable connection.

"I — what on earth are you talking about?" If she

had not known him so well, she might have been
deceived by his half-laughing, half-bewildered question.
Her eyes never left his face. There was nothing soft
about her now, nothing trusting. Her eyes probed
inexorably, searching every change of expression.

"The way you change the subject," he complained
with a laugh. "Won't you let me come in and talk? It's
not very hospitable to keep me outside the door this
way."

She did not move. "I'm not changing the subject.
"Are you Hubert King's attorney?"

"I must say — professional ethics — you don't understand these things — confidential communications."
Willis was speaking in a confused mutter.

She forced him to look at her. "Willis, you do know
Hubert King, don't you?"

"I've handled a few small professional matters for
him," he said.

"So that's how you knew his brother would be
wanting a secretary, of course."

"Well, he mentioned it, and wondered if I knew of
anyone — uh — suitable."

"Someone," Randi said, "who could be counted on to
do his work and not to be a danger to Hubert's interests? Someone who wouldn't want to marry him, in
spite of all that money? Someone already engaged to be
married and guaranteed to be deeply in love. Is that
true?"

"Randi, how can you? Naturally I thought of you
because I didn't see why you shouldn't have a chance to
earn all that salary."

"And who told you that Jonas King had asked me to marry him?"

"Why I — you can't be — you must be joking. I don't understand you at all tonight."

"I understand you for the first time."

"But I never thought — you and Jonas King —" He stammered, not knowing what to say, wincing under the open contempt in the girl's face.

"So," she went on, her voice clear and cold and steady, "when you learned that he had asked me to marry him and that he planned to change his will, something had to be done. Right away. You just happened to remember that I always stop to look at the construction. You just happened to mention it to someone who might be interested. Or were you the man with the knife who cut the rope and let the platform fall, Willis?"

He stared at her without speaking. There was no pity, no yielding in her face. Unexpectedly he said, his voice breaking, "Believe it or not, I didn't want you hurt, Randi. I didn't realize — you're so sweet. You mustn't be hurt!"

"I want you to go, Willis, and you aren't to come back."

As she started to close the door he cried desperately, "Randi, look out for yourself. You're in danger. Be very careful."

When he had gone down the steps to the street, Randi closed the door and fastened the bolt. Then she leaned against her chair, her knees buckled, she fell into it.

"Randi!" Melody cried, kneeling beside her, clutching her hand. "Oh, Randi!"

After a long time Randi said, sounding dazed, "I can't seem to get it into my head that Willis could be part of — of something like that."

"But when he heard about the scaffolding he knew the accident had been — meant for you."

"Yes," Randi agreed. "He knew. Isn't there anyone we can trust?"

ii

"To trust anyone to that extent," the lawyer said angrily, "is madness."

Jonas King smiled serenely at him. "And that is why I mean to give my entire estate to the King foundation. You may not have a high regard for my intelligence, but you know perfectly well that I am as sane as you are."

"But to put the bulk of your estate — and it will run well over six millions — in the hands of this young fellow Cary Hamilton — is too great a risk. Why, to all intents and purposes, it makes him your sole beneficiary. You are assuming that he is above human weaknesses, above temptation, that he won't want to get his hands on that money as soon as he possibly can."

"He won't." Jonas smiled at the irate lawyer. "And I am not such a fool as to believe he is above human temptations or weaknesses, but he is man enough not to yield to them."

"And this girl you are going to marry. How old is she?"

"Twenty-two."

The lawyer took a long breath and said, with as much restraint as he could muster, "And you are fifty."

Jonas smiled again, nodding his head in amiable agreement.

"How long have you known her?"

Jonas considered. "About — oh, say, two months. Perhaps a little less."

"And I suppose she has assured you that she is head over heels in love with you."

This time Jonas chuckled. "Actually she was engaged to another man until yesterday."

"When did you propose to her?"

"The day before."

Billings snorted. "There's no fool like an old fool. I feel like walking out of here and letting you find yourself another lawyer."

"You won't do that," Jonas said confidently. "In the first place, you don't walk out on old clients who depend on you."

"Clients are supposed to take advice from their lawyers. What's the point of having them, otherwise?"

"I am marrying Randi Scott for two reasons," Jonas King told him. "One is that unless I marry, there is a strong chance that Hubert not only would try to break my will but that he might — uh — hasten my demise."

"Do you know what you are saying?"

"Yes, of course I do."

"Then steps must be taken at once."

Jonas grinned at him. "Such as?" he asked gently. "I've given this matter a great deal of thought. You know I have no proof. That's why there's no sense in adding a codicil to my will pointing out my reasons for disinheriting my brother. He could go to court screaming indignantly that he had been maligned, that I have no proof. On the other hand, you know I cannot be constantly on my guard for the rest of my life. I may not have long to live, but I intend to enjoy the time I have left in some peace of mind. By marrying me, Randi will provide me with a measure of security. And," he raised his hand to forestall the lawyer's inevitable comment, "naturally I will provide security for her, a life income. Don't misunderstand me, Billings. I haven't asked for her love, only for her faith. She will give me that."

There was confidence in King's voice that silenced Billings's protests. They had known each other for twenty years, and he had rarely found that King made mistakes in his judgment of people.

"Does this girl expect that she will be coming into your whole fortune?"

"There is no deception on either side," Jonas assured the anxious lawyer. "She knows my intentions and knows that I am leaving my estate not to her but to the Foundation, which Cary Hamilton will direct."

The lawyer pushed back his chair, paced uneasily up and down the room. "What is to prevent a girl, young and I presume attractive, from trying to latch onto Hamilton as soon as she can?"

Again King smiled, this time with compassion and understanding. "If I am not mistaken, Cary is already in love with Randi, whether he knows it or not." He ignored the lawyer's loud groan of despairing protest. "There are still people of integrity in this world, Billings, even though you lose sight of them in *your* profession. I am building everything I have on those two."

"That is exactly what I object to."

Jonas laughed. "Get your witnesses and bring them in," he said. "Let's sign this document without any further discussion."

"If you are sure —"

"Quite sure," Jonas said tranquilly. He smiled again. "And I have another favor to ask of you; I want you to give away the bride." He saw the lawyer's expression of dismay and laughed aloud.

VIII

RANDI was glad that the early start for New York would enable her to get out of the house before she had to listen to a recapitulation of the accident of the day before as it had been related by Mrs. Echo's husband. Now that she was sure of Willis's part in the affair, she wanted only to forget the whole horrible business as quickly as possible.

As she understood the situation, the nurse probably had told Hubert of the proposal she had overheard. Hubert had discussed the approaching marriage with Willis. Apparently Willis had jumped immediately to the conclusion that she would accept Jonas's proposal. She wondered what he would feel if he knew that she had originally refused Jonas for his sake and had accepted him only after she knew that Willis cared for someone else. She put the thought away from her. All that belonged to the past when she had loved Willis, when she had believed their lives would be linked together forever.

Apparently Hubert had said that the marriage must be stopped. Willis — at least this was Randi's guess — had mentioned casually that Randi always stopped to look at the building under construction on Main Street. Not even to himself would he be likely to admit what he was doing or that he was laying the foundation for her being injured, perhaps fatally.

Willis was not good at facing facts, particularly about himself. He had been genuinely shocked and angry with her for accusing him of his part in the incident, but he had been genuinely terrified, too, by the fact that she had nearly been struck by the falling scaffold. For once, the true meaning of his own actions, in all their ugliness, had come home to him.

Poor Willis! Randi was sorry for him, for his weakness, for his inability to take responsibility for his own actions. But she was free of him now. Free forever. No more regrets. Only a sense of relief over her narrow escape. Suppose she had married him and discovered too late what he was like!

This morning, in preparation for the trip to New York, she wore a pale green sheath, the color of the young leaves on the weeping willows, a white wool coat and short white gloves, no hat on her black hair. For some reason she took particular pains in dressing, and stopped for a long critical scrutiny of the girl in the mirror. She did not ask herself why she wanted to look particularly nice, or why she was so happy.

There was an early morning chill in the air when she went out of doors. Cary Hamilton was waiting at the wheel of his little Renault. He had declined the use of Jonas's Buick, not willing to admit to himself that he felt he had received too many favors; anyhow, he preferred to drive Randi in a car he owned himself. He got down to open the door for her and help her in beside him.

"You look better this morning," he said after a quick glance at her glowing face. "I hope you were able to sleep after that shock."

Randi was about to tell him that she'd had a worse shock, the discovery that Willis Jameson had some share in the responsibility for bringing about the accident, that the trap had been set for her, that Willis had formed some criminal partnership with Hubert King. Then she decided to say nothing. Although she felt sure, she had no real evidence, and it was a terrible accusation. If Cary were to feel he ought to act upon it, and take steps to punish either Willis or Hubert King, it could only cause a scandal, which would do Jonas a great deal of harm and achieve little good. Anyhow, now that she was forewarned, she would be able to look after herself. Willis had meant it when he had told her that she was in danger. Perhaps he had never really loved her, as she understood love, but he must have some affection for her. He had been frightened for her. But did he know who had wielded the knife that had cut the rope? Randi was not sure she wanted to know the answer to that question.

The little car went down a long hill while Randi pointed out beds of daffodils, tulips, flowering magnolias, and flowering quince, delighting in the loveliest spring she had ever known. Beside her Cary drove in silence, competently, his eyes on the road.

Now and then, stealing a shy look at him, Randi realized that his whole attention seemed to be on his driving, his eyes moving constantly from the road to the rear-view mirror.

"Do you know anyone who drives a cream Pontiac?" he asked unexpectedly.

She shook her head. "I can't think of anyone in particular. Why?"

"There's one right on my tail; I can't seem to shake it off. I wondered if it could be someone following you."

Randi's heart stopped, raced on. "Oh, no! Suppose he tries again!"

Having given herself away, she was forced, by Cary's insistent questions, to tell him the whole story, beginning with Hubert putting the nurse in Jonas's house as his spy. Apparently Mavis had told Hubert of overhearing Jonas's proposal. He had found out somehow — Randi gulped, and decided to leave out Willis's shameful part in the affair — that she always stopped to watch the new building under construction, and so the accident had been staged.

If it had not been for the rope, which had been cut with a knife, Cary would have been inclined to dismiss the whole story as incredible. As it was, he turned it over in his mind.

"Do you really believe that Mr. King's brother is trying to get you out of the way?"

"Not on my account particularly, but because he wants Jonas's money."

Cary said, his voice expressionless, "And you would like to see a new will put into effect."

"Well, of course I would! It just has to! Jonas is doing the best, the very wisest, thing he can do with his money."

Cary laughed without amusement. "You and this Hubert seem to be two very determined characters. It will be interesting to see which of you wins out."

"There is only one possible victory here," Randi said crisply, "and that is the successful carrying out of Jonas's wishes."

"And what," Cary asked almost lazily, almost indifferently, "do you plan to do with all that money?"

It was a long moment before Randi understood his meaning, and felt his contempt and distrust cut through her like a sharp knife. The brightness went out of the sky, out of the day.

"Why you — you —" she sputtered. She fought for control. "You think that I am marrying Jonas for his money, that I am ready to fight his own family just — just to get my hands on it. The residuary legatee, Mr. Hamilton, is the King Foundation. And Jonas wants *you* to have charge of his house and his fortune to enable you to carry on your work. Because he believes in the work; he believes in you. I thought you knew that."

The car rolled down the Sawmill River Parkway, began to pick up a little traffic, and always the Pontiac maintained its position about three car lengths behind the Renault.

Cary's thoughts were in a turmoil. Now he understood what Jonas King had meant when he had said
that he would be concerned in the future. There was no
time to think of the fortune that would eventually come
into his control, only a realization of the depth of the
trust Jonas had imposed in him.

He was aware, too, of the injury he had done the girl
beside him. He looked down at the cap of shining black
hair and longed to touch it, wondering if it could
possibly be as soft as it seemed. He looked at the
smoldering face. She was bitterly angry with him and
she had a right to be.

The car stopped for a toll station, went down the
Henry Hudson Parkway, the great river sparkling in
the sun, a couple of freighters lying at anchor, the
George Washington Bridge soaring above. On the left
and ahead rose the massive towers of the most important city in the world.

There must be something he could say, Cary thought
in despair, to repair the insult he had implied, his
assumption that she was marrying King for his money,
when instead she was delighted that it was to go to
Cary. The trouble, he admitted to himself, was that he
was afraid to say anything for fear he would say too
much, be led on to tell her that he loved her. And
Jonas's trust made that impossible. Unless — unless it
might be a kind of anchor to know she had him to
depend on, particularly if she were right and Hubert
was determined to prevent the marriage at any cost.

He recalled vividly the moment when the scaffold

had crashed on the spot where, seconds before, the defenseless girl had stood rooted. He remembered his discovery that the rope had not broken, it had been cut. Now the persistence of the Pontiac in trailing them took on new significance. Randi Scott was in danger.

Cary slowed for an exit, drove through heavy, noisy traffic across town, through Central Park, started down Fifth Avenue.

"Please let me out here," Randi said coldly. "I'll take care of my shopping and go home by myself."

"Randi! Randi, forgive me. Randi, please."

A traffic officer blew his whistle. "Look," Cary said desperately, "you can't leave me like this. I'll drop you at Tiffany's, park the car, and come back to meet you there. That's what Mr. King asked. Please, Randi. For his sake."

"All right," she agreed, the happy lilt gone, her voice lifeless.

When he had let her out in front of the famous jewelry store, the Renault moved on, slid into traffic. Behind it came the cream Pontiac. At the wheel was a heavyset man who seemed vaguely familiar. Then Randi remembered. The man who had been following them so assiduously was Hubert King.

ii

Whatever the emotions of the young couple might be, it was essential that they appear normal, that all indications of emotional stress should be under control when they met at Tiffany's to purchase the rings Jonas wanted for his wife and the groom's gift for his bride.

A clerk who had been instructed personally by Jonas over the telephone greeted them, smiling, and led them to the proper counter.

After looking at Randi he said warmly, "Mr. King is to be congratulated. I am sorry to hear that he is not able to come to New York himself at the moment, but I feel confident we can find something that will satisfy him — and you too, of course, Miss Scott."

With Cary standing beside her, she agreed to the wedding ring that Jonas had described by telephone. Personally she would have preferred a simple band, but the ring he wanted her to have was diamond-studded. The clerk stood back and waited for Cary to slip the ring on her slender finger to judge the size.

For a moment Randi looked up into Cary's face, into his burning eyes. Why, I love him, she discovered. That is why his distrust could hurt me so terribly. I love him. *This is my real marriage.* Then, her eyes wide with shock which he could not understand, she pushed the thought away.

The engagement ring took longer to select. Randi insisted on a small stone and the clerk was distressed.

"I am sure, from the way Mr. King spoke," he told her, "that he had in mind something more —"

"More lavish?" Randi asked, and found Cary watching her closely.

"More beautiful perhaps," the clerk said tactfully. "Now this stone, you see —"

The stone seemed much too large, almost ostentatious, Randi thought. Somehow it was not like Jonas and his essentially simple tastes. Then she realized that this was his way of trying to compensate for the fact that her marriage was not to be like other marriages. At length she agreed to take the ring with the bigger diamond. She tried it on. But this time she did not look up at Cary. She kept her eyes steadily on the big stone that reflected multicolored lights. Curious how heavy the ring felt, as though it were a chain binding her.

"Mr. King," the clerk said happily, feeling that he was fulfilling a valued client's wishes, "also was most particular about the groom's gift for the bride. He suggested a diamond bracelet unless, of course, Miss Scott has some other preference."

"A diamond bracelet! It's too much! Must I?" she exclaimed in distress, turning instinctively to Cary for advice and support.

He took half a step toward her and then checked himself with a visible effort. "Yes, I think so." His voice was restrained. "It will give him a great deal of pleasure, you know."

The clerk looked from one revealing face to the other. These two were obviously in love with each other, deeply and completely in love. Yet the girl was marrying someone else and the tall young man was acting as a kind of stand-in for the bridegroom.

The situation was beyond his experience and he did not know how to handle it. As a rule there was enormous satisfaction in selling engagement rings because the couple was so happy. But something here was terribly wrong.

He brought out half a dozen diamond bracelets, one at a time, and set them down on black velvet. At length the reluctant bride picked up one of them. "This one, I think," she said. Passively she let Cary fasten it on a slim wrist, watched it glitter in the light.

"I can't wear it this afternoon. I'll just be shopping. Perhaps you can have it delivered."

"Of course." The clerk produced a professional smile and bowed them out. He stared after the silent young couple. It's not my business, he reminded himself, but he shook his head dubiously.

IX

"LET'S have lunch at the Gotham," Cary suggested. "Afterwards I know you'll have shopping to do, but I'll meet you wherever you like when you've finished."

"Fine," she said listlessly.

When they had ordered she sat staring at the big diamond that glittered on her ring finger.

"You hate that, don't you?" Cary said abruptly. "The rings, the bracelet —"

She made no reply, but she was careful not to risk lifting betraying eyes to his face. Only that morning he had suggested that she was marrying Jonas in order to get her greedy hands on his fortune. He had changed his mind about that. At least he knew that the money was destined for him, not for her. But had she betrayed herself, her uncontrollable feeling for him, in that moment when he had slipped the ring on her finger? She felt the blood burning in her cheeks and she was helpless to prevent the blush.

"Why are you marrying Jonas King, Randi?" Cary demanded.

"That doesn't concern you."

"It concerns me more than I could make you believe,

more than I am in a position to tell you. Jonas King is
the best friend I've ever had; he has done a great deal
for me. I can't fail him now. But if you aren't happy in
this marriage — it's not too late to change your mind."

Shrimp cocktails came and she was spared the immediate need to reply. Then she said, "Jonas trusts me
as he trusts you. Completely. Perhaps I can prolong his
life and stand as a barrier between him and his brother.
I can bring him a sort of happiness, laughter and
gaiety, and cheer up that gloomy old house. I can help
in this strange way — but we can't always choose our
way to serve — to fight the battle for children's minds,
to keep them free and proud of their freedom instead of
afraid of it, as some people would like them to be. I can
make sure that none of Jonas's money is used to support that ugly cause."

The bowls of ice that had held the shrimp cocktails
were removed, veal scallopine and tiny browned potatoes and asparagus took their place.

"Randi," Cary said at last, "forgive me if you can for
what I said while we were driving down."

"You didn't know. I suppose it was the natural
conclusion for you to draw. A great many people will
probably believe the same thing. It's one of life's most
familiar comic situations, isn't it? The aging man
tricked by a young woman. But I can't let what people
think influence me as long as I feel I am doing the right
thing, the only possible thing, in the circumstances."

"I should have known the truth. The moment I saw
you I found the girl I've been looking for, and the next

moment I discovered that she belonged to someone else, to my best friend."

The big brown eyes were looking into his gray ones now.

"I love you, Randi," he said steadily, "but I know there is no chance for me. And like you, I don't want to hurt or endanger Jonas. I am telling you this only because I want you to know that there is someone you can depend on, call upon in time of need. But I am going away. I — there's a limit to what a man can endure. I'll never ask anything of you, but just remember always that this is love with honor. You have only to call, only to say a word, and I will be there to help."

"I know," she said huskily. She blinked tears away from her lashes.

"Can you —" he began and checked himself. "I have no right to ask."

"More coffee for Madame?" asked the waiter.

Randi was in a turmoil. Cary loved her. Loved her! Whatever happened to her for all the rest of her life, she had this moment to remember. But it was love with honor. She had set her feet on this path and she must go on to the end of the journey.

Cary was waiting for her to speak, and she did not dare answer the question he had hesitated to ask. What could she say? That the moment they had met, the moment his hand had touched hers, she had felt as though she had come home? That an hour before, when he had slipped the ring on her finger, she had recognized this as her real marriage?

She must say none of these things. She must guard her tongue lest she be carried away into some indiscretion. She began to talk quickly, almost aimlessly. "Cary, I know who was driving that cream Pontiac."

"Pontiac?" His thoughts were so far away that he had to pull them back with an effort. "Oh, yes, the man who seemed to be trailing us."

"I think that is just what he was doing," Randi told him, and now Cary's attention came back with a rush. "I recognized him when he followed you on Fifth Avenue. That was Jonas's younger brother, Hubert King. He —" She was looking past his shoulder, still hesitant about meeting his probing, intent gray eyes. Her own eyes widened. "Cary!"

"What is it?"

"Hubert! He is sitting just behind you right this very minute."

His voice was quiet, steadying. "Do you think he knows you have seen and recognized him?"

"I don't think so. He is ordering, speaking to the waiter, looking at the menu."

"I'll get my check in a hurry and we'll try to shake him off. Randi, darling, don't look so frightened!"

She managed a tremulous smile. "At least there is no scaffolding here. Now," she added quickly, as the waiter came to their table, "get your check, pay it, and let's get out. Hubert is looking at us now, but if we are careful and quick I think we can manage it."

She timed their movements, watching without appearing to do so the heavyset man at the table behind theirs. Cary paid his bill. Randi waited until a waiter brought soup to Hubert's table and a large party at the back of the restaurant began to approach their own table.

"As they pass we can get up and Hubert won't even notice until we have gone."

They mingled with the crowd, hastened out of the restaurant, through the lobby. Randi wanted to look back and see whether they were being followed, but Cary rushed her along, his hand on her arm.

"Don't let him know we have spotted him," he said, and gave an exclamation of relief when he found a taxi waiting outside the hotel where it had just discharged some passengers. He risked a glance behind him but there was no sign of Hubert. He leaned back in the seat grinning. "He'd have been rather conspicuous if he had rushed out after us just as he began to eat his lunch!" Cary laughed. "He doesn't look like a man who misses meals if he can help it. At least I hope we spoiled his appetite."

As the taxi moved away from the curb he said, "Please tell me what you plan to do this afternoon."

"I want to go to Bergdorf-Goodman. Jonas opened an account for me there and I'll do what shopping must be done for the — the wedding at that one store."

"Then I'm going with you," he declared, and he insisted on following her into the store. "I don't like to let you out of my sight," he groaned. "It begins to look as though you were right and the man means business."

"Well, you'll have to let me out of sight when I try

on clothes," Randi said, "but just remember that if you can't follow me into a fitting room, he can't either." She tried to speak more confidently than she felt.

"I'll wait right here," Cary said firmly, sitting rather awkwardly beside her on one of the small gilt chairs for customers who are having clothes modeled for them.

Randi watched the models pass, aware that other customers as well as the helpful clerk believed that she and Cary were engaged, that he was the man who had provided the diamond that flashed on her finger, that it was for his pleasure that she was selecting a trousseau.

Recalling what she knew of Jonas's tastes, she chose evening dresses, afternoon dresses, sportswear, a yellow chiffon negligee with matching slippers and another of white velvet. For her wedding dress she selected a simple, floor-length dress of princess satin, without a train. Her mother's rose-point veil had been carefully put away for Melody and Randi, but Randi could not bear to wear it for this marriage. She chose instead a simple off-the-face lace cap with a short veil.

Beside her, Cary watched the model in the wedding dress, eyes downcast, walking slowly across the floor, turning, advancing, retreating. He wondered if any other man had ever been subjected to such torture. In a few days Randi, his lovely Randi, Jonas's lovely Randi, would move across a room in that white dress, walking toward an altar where she would pledge her troth to another man. And she would steadfastly keep her vows.

Randi pushed back in her mind the longing, realizing that this beautiful wardrobe was for another kind of marriage. No regrets, she told herself fiercely. She couldn't abandon Jonas to Hubert's tender mercies, leave him to shift for himself, not while his brother was determined to get what he wanted, no matter how great or how terrible the cost. Nonetheless, while she tried on the wedding dress in the fitting room, she found her rebellious heart wishing that she could wear it to meet Cary at the altar instead of Jonas.

When she had ordered the clothes sent to Jonas's house she took the elevator down to find Cary waiting, his face rather red as amused customers kept looking at him, models strutted for his benefit rather than that of the would-be buyers, and more than one woman looked enviously at the man she took for a happy bridegroom.

He wanted — how he wanted — to have this one evening with Randi. Jonas himself had suggested it. Why shouldn't he allow himself this great happiness? But he knew why he shouldn't. It would be an act of broken faith. And suppose Randi — no, he would not let himself think what it would mean if she returned his love.

"Ready?" he asked and she nodded. "Jonas suggested that we do a theater and dinner and perhaps dance for a while tonight. I don't think that's a good idea, Randi. I'm not made of steel filings. I suggest that we go back home. Is that all right with you?"

She nodded without speaking. Then she saw his sudden change of expression. "What is worrying you, Cary?"

"I was just wondering about the safest way of getting you home," he said, his voice grim.

She looked around quickly. "Hubert? I don't see him."

"He doesn't need to wait here. If he's the man with the cream Pontiac, he followed me to the garage I always use in New York. All he has to do is to wait there for us to show up."

Randi drew a quick, unsteady breath. "Then I am endangering you too. It was stupid of me not to realize that before now."

"I can take care of myself. Well, there's no point in hanging around here. Let's go." Once outside the store he drew a long breath of air in relief. "Whew! Am I glad to get out of there! Women!" He said it with such heartfelt relief that Randi burst into a gale of laughter, and with her laughter the brightness came back to the sky and it was spring again, in her heart as well as in the world around her.

ii

Cary gripped her arm tightly when they went into the garage, stood between her and the doorway while he waited for cars to be shuffled around and the Renault to be driven down the ramp, took advantage of split-second timing to move into traffic and onto the West Side Highway. Then he relaxed, only to stiffen in alarm when Randi said, "Did you see him?"

"Hubert? No! Did you?"

"Yes, he was standing back in the shadows of the little cubbyhole office, looking out while they were shifting cars. I think," her voice trembled, steadied again, "that he is probably close behind us now. I saw him signal and hold out his ticket as I was getting into the car."

Commuting traffic moved at a fair clip but it was almost bumper to bumper, and Cary's attention was fully engrossed, watching his own lane, keeping an eye on merging traffic, allowing for the sudden turns of drivers who neglected to put on their directional signals.

"I don't see the Pontiac," he said finally, watching the rear-view mirror, "but there are so darned many cars it's hard to tell. All I'm sure of is that he isn't behind us in this lane."

Beyond the turnoff for the George Washington Bridge traffic began to thin out. By the time they had reached Hawthorne Circle there was only a trickle of cars left, for only diehard suburbanites like to live so far from their work. Most of the cars now were in the oncoming traffic, southbound, headed for Manhattan and a gay evening.

Cary found his mind lingering on a picture of an evening spent with this radiant girl at his side. Dinner and a theater and dancing. He had never danced with her. Once he let his imagination free, he could visualize other evenings, not spent in a search for gaiety and entertainment, but quiet evenings, watching the crackle of flames in a fireplace, watching stars in a clear sky. Evenings when there was no need to rush into speech because there would be time for all that, infinite time, the rest of their lives.

Stop it, you fool! he told himself savagely. You'll

only make matters worse for yourself, make it more painful to leave her, to step out of her life entirely. And that's what you —

He snapped back to attention, wrenched the wheel over hard, stepped on the gas, bumped over a curb. The cream Pontiac shot past like a rocket, almost grazing the Renault, which was shaken by the force of its passing.

Randi stifled a cry. "What — what happened?"

"He tried to sideswipe the car, to turn us over." Cary's jaw clenched with fury. "If this had been a narrow road, with no place to turn off, he'd have succeeded. We were sitting ducks. His car is heavy and this one is so light it would have folded like an accordion. Oh, Randi!"

Her hand clutched his arm, slipped down to find his hand, clung to it. He held it firmly in his, and then under her white kid glove he felt the bulge of her engagement ring. He released the brake, eased the car over the curb, and slid back into his lane again.

"It's all right now. He can't get back for some time. He'll have to drive a dozen blocks before he can get on the highway again. We'll make it home safely."

"Cary?"

"Yes, my —" He bit off the endearment.

"We mustn't tell Jonas. It will only frighten him, worry him needlessly."

"We won't tell Jonas," he agreed, "but I'll find someone to whom I can tell the whole story: Jonas's lawyer, the state police, someone in authority who will see that this thing stops and that you are protected. I was a fool to think I could do it single-handed."

"It's only for a few days," she reminded him. "Once the will is signed and Jonas and I are married, there will be no harm that anyone can do. Nothing can possibly happen in four days, can it?"

Cary, his eyes moving from the road to the rear-view mirror, his hands tightening on the wheel, made no reply.

X

THE little guesthouse was quiet at last, which meant that a reluctant Andy had finally gone to sleep, fighting every yawn, standing determinedly in his bed until his tired legs crumpled under him. John Lancing stood looking down at his sleeping son, at the tight gold curls, the red cheeks, the mouth that was so touching in sleep. What was going to happen to this small son of his? What would Helen think of the way he was being allowed to scream for his own way until he got it?

He sighed, switched out the light in the little bedroom, and went down to the living room. For many months his grief for Helen had been an unending ache. Even now loneliness enclosed him when he settled in a deep comfortable chair before the cheerful fire that was made pleasant by the cool spring night. Cary had been lucky to have this charming guesthouse turned over to him for as long as he cared to live in it. Everything a man could possibly want was here: comfort and beauty and privacy. Everything but a woman's touch.

Perhaps, John Lancing thought, Cary was not so lucky after all. There was no question that he had fallen in love with Randi Scott and it had been a terrible blow to him to discover that she was going to marry Jonas King. It was curious about Randi, John thought. She certainly had not struck him as the kind of girl who would marry for wealth rather than love. There was a directness, an honesty about her that — hang it all, it just wasn't possible. And yet, fine as Jonas King was, he doubted that the girl was in love with him.

His mind shifted from Randi to her sister. Melody! That day she had handled Andy so smoothly that he was not even aware that he was being managed. When he had shouted she had said mildly that she could not hear him until he lowered his voice. Where he had been accustomed to demanding, he was already learning to ask. As the youngest child in the group he found himself unable to lead or give orders to the Brooks children. If he was to play with them at all, he had to play according to their rules. All in all, it had been a good day. A wonderful day.

Perhaps it had not been necessary, John admitted with a grin, for him to spend so much of the time at the Scott cottage. He had explained to Melody, more carefully than was necessary, that he wanted to see for himself how her methods worked out. He wondered whether he had fooled her any more than he had himself.

Helen and Melody. There was no disloyalty. He had loved his wife devotedly. He had mourned her deeply. But there was an empty place in his heart, in his life, and Melody . . .

Hey, he warned himself, you are going too fast. You

have seen this girl only twice. Then he remembered Shakespeare's, "Who ever loved that loved not at first sight?"

He closed the book he was holding open on his lap and leaned back in his chair, letting himself dream of a golden-haired girl with an exquisite face and dark-lashed blue eyes.

When the door opened, letting in a blast of cold air, he turned around, startled, to see Cary.

"Hello there! I thought you were going to spend the night at your club in New York!" he exclaimed. His expression changed. "My God, Cary! What happened?"

"Someone tried it again," Cary said tightly.

"Tried what?"

"To kill Randi."

After an incredulous moment, John said, "You had better sit down and tell me about it, hadn't you?"

"Yes, I think it's time someone knew about this, in case the next attempt succeeds."

Cary started with the way Hubert King had tried to hasten his brother's death so that he could get hold of his money for subversive purposes, how he had planted the nurse in the house to report what was going on. He went on, his face impassive, to say that Jonas had asked Randi to marry him and that he was going to draw up a new will, if he had not already done so, in order to prevent Hubert from getting the money.

"It sounds like a soap opera," John commented. "I can't believe it."

"You had better believe it." Cary was grim. "You

yourself saw the scaffolding fall when Randi was right under it."

"But —"

"I told you at the time the rope had been cut, John. Someone knew Randi would stop to look at the construction. She always did. The DANGER sign had been moved out of the way so she would walk down the sidewalk. Someone with a knife must have waited until she was on the right spot."

"Have you had any dinner?" John asked casually.

"Dinner? No, I — we had lunch at the Gotham. I — it seemed best to come home." While John was getting ready toast, coffee, and scrambled eggs, Cary described his near-fatal collision with Hubert on the Sawmill River Parkway.

John then put the food on a small table beside Cary. "Tuck into that," he said. "We'll talk later, but you need to look after the inner man first."

When Cary had finished he looked up to say with a smile, "Thanks, John. I didn't know how much I needed some food. I feel better able to cope now." He filled his pipe and leaned back in his chair, relaxed, rested, the harsh strain gone from his face.

"So what it boils down to," John said at length, after thinking it over, "is that we have got to protect both Randi and Mr. King until after the marriage and the signing of the new will."

"But we can't," Cary pointed out, "warn Jonas King about the extent of his danger, because our principal need at this point is to save him from any further emotional shocks. And how we can protect him without his knowing it is beyond me. As for Randi —"

"To begin with," John said, "you needn't worry about what happens to Randi on her way back and forth to work until she is married. I'll be taking Andy to her sister every morning. I can walk back with Randi and reverse the process in the evening, escort her home and bring Andy back. No one would have a chance to get at her."

"Thanks, John. That — thanks a lot."

For the first time John's serious expression was transformed by his smile, the same one that was in danger of being Andy's downfall. "I'm speaking one word for you and two for myself," he admitted. "Sitting here tonight I've been thinking ahead, thinking of that empty house in Phoenix; in short, well, if I could persuade Melody Scott to go back there as my wife I'd be the luckiest fellow on earth and Andy would be in good hands."

"I wish you all the luck in the world, John," Cary told him. "She's an exquisite creature. I — man was not born to live alone."

"I'll need all the luck I can get to persuade her to marry me," John said. "But that's enough about my affairs. The immediate thing is the problem of Randi's safety, and King's. I can protect her when she is going back and forth. But in the house — I don't see what we can do to guard either of them there. Even if we alert the servants —"

"And if we were to do that the news would be all

over the village within twenty-four hours," Cary said.
"Some of them go home nights and they are bound to
gossip with their families. The only one who might be
useful to us is Luther. He is devoted to Mr. King. At
least one good thing is that Mavis Bertram will be out
of a job. If we could replace her by a nurse whom we
could trust, someone who would be constantly on
guard, we could almost guarantee Mr. King's safety."

"I have a better idea than that," John said suddenly.
He began to grin. Rapidly he outlined his plan.

"Of all the Machiavellian suggestions!" Cary
laughed. "There's not a chance that it would work out,
that they would fall for it."

"Want to bet?" John said.

ii

An hour later, when Cary had called Jonas's housekeeper and arranged to have the cook act as baby-sitter
for Andy, the two men set out. John Lancing went to
lay the groundwork for the plan that had so amused
Cary. The latter got out his little car and, having
verified the address of Jonas King's lawyer, he released
the brake and let the car roll gently down the curving
driveway onto the road before starting the motor.

The lawyer lived in a flawless saltbox on Main
Street, facing the Green. For a moment Cary sat in his
car, admiring the lovely lines of the old house. Then he
locked the car, went up the steps, and rang the bell.

After several rings the door was opened by a portly

man of middle age, somewhat bald, reading glasses shoved up on his forehead, an irascible expression on his face. He wore a warm dressing gown and he had his finger in a book.

"Well?" he demanded.

"Mr. Billings?"

"Yes, I'm Billings."

"I'd like very much to have a few minutes of your time."

"Time! Do you know what time it is, young man?" Billings glared at him. "Nearly ten o'clock. I keep office hours like other civilized men. If you want an appointment, you can call my secretary in the morning. But I don't talk business at this hour of the night."

Cary did not move. "Sorry, sir. I wouldn't have disturbed you if it hadn't seemed to me that even one day's delay could be too risky. The situation is dangerous enough without delays of any kind."

"Dangerous! Have you been drinking?"

"Dangerous to your client, Jonas King." As Billings continued to glare at him, Cary added, "My name is Hamilton. Cary Hamilton."

"Well, come in, come in." Billings stepped back and waved impatiently toward the living room on one side of a charming entrance hallway out of which a beautiful staircase soared. "Keep as quiet as you can. My wife's in bed and I don't want her disturbed." In the living room he indicated a chair and sat down, scowling.

"So you are Hamilton." The lawyer sat frankly studying the young man. Cary sustained the look coolly, without flinching, though he could feel color hot in his cheeks.

It's a good face, the lawyer admitted to himself in some surprise. A lot of intelligence, plenty of character. If it weren't for the way he has wormed his way into Jonas's confidence, I would call him a man of high integrity. I suppose he is here because he simply can't bear the suspense and wants to know about that new will Jonas signed today.

"Well?" he demanded. "You seemed to be in one deuce of a hurry, barging in on a man at ten o'clock at night. No appointment. Nothing. Can't even wait until morning. What is it all about? What do you want of me?"

Cary answered the second question first. "I don't quite know," he admitted. "Advice, for one thing. To go on record about the situation as I understand it, for another. And third — or perhaps first — help."

"Go ahead." Billings leaned back, fitted his fingertips together, listened, his eyes never leaving the face of this tall young stranger.

"I suppose," Cary began, "that Mr. King has already informed you of his engagement and approaching marriage to Randi Scott and of the fact that he intends to make a new will."

Billings merely looked at him. He made no reply. For twenty-five years he had guarded the secrets and confidences of his clients and he did not intend to change his ways now for this confident and probably unscrupulous young man.

"I've come to you, sir, because something has got to be done," Cary said, "to protect Mr. King and Miss Scott until they are married and that will is signed."

Whatever he had expected, it was not this. The lawyer sat bolt upright. "Just what are you getting at?"

"Apparently, Mr. King's brother Hubert has his eyes on the King fortune and he is not squeamish about how he gets it. He has tried several times to shock Mr. King into a heart attack; and there have been two deliberate attempts in the last two days to kill Miss Scott."

"What's that!" The words came out like an explosion. Then, with an anxious look toward the staircase for fear he had disturbed his wife, the lawyer said, attempting to pull himself together and to speak calmly, "I think you had better explain."

Cary did so. When the long detailed recital had ended the lawyer sat frowning. "Why did you come to me?"

"I thought I had explained that in the beginning. If something should — happen to me there would be no one in a position of authority to act. My friend Lancing can protect Miss Scott as she goes back and forth. He has an idea that may — I can only say may — work by providing some kind of security inside the house. But it isn't enough, sir."

"What do you suggest?"

"I have no authority. What I hope you will do is to inform the state police. Make clear to them that this is a matter that must not be made public, but that they must keep a careful eye on Hubert King and his associates, whoever they are. Personally, I think you'll find most of them in the All-American Party."

As Billings made a muffled exclamation, Cary nodded grimly.

"Twice Hubert has missed his objective by seconds, by inches." His face was white. He wiped his forehead and the palms of his hands with his handkerchief. "I don't want to live through anything like that again. Actually I might not be so lucky a third time. That is why it is essential to have reinforcements. If I am put out of the running, I'd like to know there is someone to replace me."

He started to put back the handkerchief, felt the small box in his pocket, drew it out. He held it for a moment, turning it over and over, unopened. It was the box containing Randi's wedding ring. Then he returned it to his pocket.

"Well, sir?" he asked at length.

"Give me ten minutes to change. I'll go to the state police with you."

While the lawyer trotted upstairs, Cary leaned back and drew a long breath of relief. For some reason Billings did not like him, did not even trust him; but at least he had believed his story and he was prepared to do everything in his power to protect Jonas King.

The two men drove without further talk to the state police barracks, where two men in trim uniforms and one in plain clothes were drinking coffee, making out reports, answering the telephone. Apparently Billings was known, because the lieutenant, whose name was

Barker, got up to shake hands and greet him by name. Billings introduced Cary.

The lieutenant's face lighted up with pleasure. "I heard your talk on television the other night. I wish we had more people talking like that. More people in favor of getting on with the job than settling for just howling. If I never see another demonstrator's placard again, it will be too soon."

He introduced a sergeant and a trooper, and ordered more coffee. "Well, Mr. Billings, what can we do for you?"

His genial smile faded when the lawyer replied gravely, "I hope you can save a life."

iii

Once more Cary repeated his story. There was a long silence after he had finished.

"Of course," the lieutenant said, when he had roused himself from a period of brooding when no one ventured to interrupt his chain of thought, "there isn't a lot we can do unless we establish an obvious stakeout." He put up his hand as both Billings and Cary attempted to protest. "No, I realize that would be bad for Mr. King." He brooded again. "One thing we can do is to check at once on the business of that rope which dropped the swing stage. There has been a lot of talk about it. People are protesting to the contractors; the workmen are threatening to strike unless they are guaranteed more security. We'll do that first."

He set down his coffee cup. "Then we'll keep a discreet eye on Mr. Hubert King and his associates. If there is any link with the organization that is trying to undermine our school kids, I want to find it. I've got a boy in junior high who is coming home with some of the worst ideas I ever heard of. But I can't trace back their source."

He leaned forward. "Next, we'll check on this nurse, Mavis Bertram, and see what we can find on her. We'll check the license number of Hubert King's car. Of course, you understand, whether he owns a cream Pontiac or not, we have no evidence of any attempt to injure you or Miss Scott. Nothing that anyone could take into court. Just your word against his. Right, Mr. Hamilton?"

"Right," Cary agreed gloomily.

"And we'll look up this girl, Randi Scott, see what her background is."

"Miss Scott is not involved in any conspiracy," Cary said hotly. "She is the victim of one."

The lieutenant gave him a long thoughtful look and then he exchanged a quick questioning glance with Billings. Well, well, there was more here than met the eye. Hamilton appeared to take a lot of interest in his benefactor's future wife. The lawyer seemed to be aware of the situation too, and he was studying young Hamilton suspiciously.

The lieutenant stood up. "You may rest assured that we will do everything in our power to protect Mr. King. Jonas King represents just about the best we have, not only in this village or this state, but everywhere. It may be old-fashioned and sentimental to say it, but he is a truly good man. Somehow, with a man like that, the last thing you would expect is — murder."

iv

"But I didn't expect murder," Willis Jameson said. He finished the highball Hubert King had poured him, and shoved his glass back for a refill. "I didn't for a single minute expect violence. There's no need for it. A crazy and criminal way to behave. Besides," he added weakly, "you might be caught."

"Tell it to the Marines," Hubert said impatiently. "How come you just happened to tell me that Randi Scott went past that building at such a time every day and stopped to look at the construction? What did you think I was going to do with that little piece of information after Mavis came to report that King was going to marry the girl?"

"I didn't know you would take a chance on — hurting her, or — well, it could have been murder."

"Accident is the operative word," Hubert told him. "Little Lord Fauntleroy, all dewy innocence! I must say I picked myself two lousy helpers." His small eyes surveyed Willis and the tall blond woman who was listening sullenly to the talk. "Two people who were going to share with me in one of the biggest plums around anywhere. Six million bucks. Six million." He licked his lips. "And what happens? Willis," and he let his voice rise to a ludicrous falsetto, "didn't know what he was doing. He didn't know the poor little girl must be removed from our path."

He swiveled around in his chair. "And as for you, Mavis, you must have loused it up somehow. How did you manage to get yourself fired today? Aside from what Jonas paid you, I've given you plenty. Plenty. Know what that emerald ring cost? And you haven't earned a cent of it so far. Just when you could be useful you get fired. You can't even hold a job."

"That's not fair," Mavis protested. "I did try. I did everything I could to make the poor man comfortable."

Hubert chuckled and she flushed with anger.

"Well, anyhow," she said defensively, "I can't see what more I could have done. I was the one who heard him propose to that fool girl, wasn't I? Where would you be if I hadn't picked up that information for you? Out on a limb, that's where you would be. First thing you know, your brother would be married and it would be too late to do anything about the situation then."

"And then he fired you. Why?"

"I don't know."

Hubert reached out a brutal hand, twisted her arm so that she cried out. Willis took a half step forward and then set his lips, but he made no protest, he did not attempt to interfere. Looking at him, the girl saw that he would be of no real help in time of trouble. Willis would look after Willis first. She had always known that, known that he would never do anything for her if it cost him anything; knew that he could not be trusted. And yet, in spite of everything, she found him the most

attractive man she knew. There must be some way to
have Willis and have money too. There had to be some
way.

And yet, for the only time in her tumultuous life, she
thought of marriage with a man like Jonas King not as
a shortcut to wealth but as a harbor of peace. Jonas
would always be kind. It would be something to know
kindness and trust in her life instead of endless plotting,
double-crossing, uncertainty.

It was a curious moment of insight into real values,
and then Mavis dismissed it as nonsense. If you were
smart you got ahead; there was no time for softness, no
place for unselfish kindness. You had to be tough to win
out.

"Why?" Hubert said again. And again he twisted
her arm. Again she cried out in pain and protest.

"Because he said I was impertinent, insolent," the
nurse said sullenly.

"Why?" It seemed to be the only word in Hubert's
vocabulary. She wanted to scream at him but she was
caught in the mesh of her own actions.

"I told Randi Scott she was very clever to get him,
or something like that, and your brother said he would
not require my services any longer."

"Yeah." For a long time Hubert watched her, his
lips nibbling like a rabbit's. "Yeah. So why were you
rude to the lady? Oh, I get it. You've been playing a
hand of your own, haven't you, Mavis baby? Had an
eye on Jonas's money all for your pretty self? Going to
marry him and cut out brother Hubert, weren't you?"

He released her arm, flung her away so that she nearly fell. "So we come back to you, Willis. I offered you fifty thousand, after the will is probated and the money comes through, to help me carry this thing out. So far you haven't done a thing to earn that money. Your bright ideas haven't worked out. Every single one of them has boomeranged. And believe me, no tickee, no washee. What made you so sure your girl wouldn't drop you for King if she had a chance at him and his money?"

"She didn't. That is —"

Hubert's eyes narrowed, moved from his face to Mavis's. "Oh! Quite a little tangle we've got. So Mavis not only tries to get Jonas for herself but she wants you too. A kind of side line." He laughed. "That's about all you're good for. What happened? Did your girl find you two together?"

His fist crashed on the table. "You fools! Neither of you has a scrap of judgment. Well, Jameson, have you any more ideas? The next one had better work."

Willis tossed back the long lock of hair from his forehead. "Randi isn't in love with the guy," he said. "I'm the man she loves. I should know. She has waited patiently for two years while I kept stalling her off."

"Why did you?" Hubert asked. "She's pretty enough, from what I've seen of her around town. Pretty? She and her sister are raving beauties."

"No money," Willis said. "I can't afford to be tied down with a gal who hasn't any money."

"I asked you before. Do you have any ideas? So far

you've made a mess of things. Our plan is queered for fair unless we work fast. That marriage must not take place. So far I don't believe the girl is likely to have made any link in her mind between that scaffolding accident and the attempt to sideswipe her this evening. They both look like straight accidents. But naturally she is going to be more on her guard, more aware of danger."

"You aren't on guard against the people you love," Willis said, and tossed back his hair again. The look of confidence was back on his face until he met Mavis's mocking eyes across the room.

"Watch your step," she told him.

"What do you mean?" Hubert asked, looking from one to the other in suspicion. He was aware that either or both of his confederates would double-cross him if they should find it profitable to do so.

Mavis smiled. "Willis is inclined to be — impulsive. I was just warning him to look out for squalls."

XI

"AREN'T you going to be late?" Melody asked in surprise.

Randi shook her head. "I'm waiting for Mr. Lancing. He is going to bring Andy here and then walk back with me."

"He really thinks you are in danger, doesn't he?" Melody said anxiously. "What happened yesterday? You were so tired last night I didn't like to ask questions."

Randi told her about the attempt to wreck Cary's car.

"Was Willis driving the other car?" Melody asked.

"Willis! No, it was Hubert King himself. I don't believe Willis could possibly do a thing like that."

"Randi Scott, you aren't still defending him, are you?"

Randi shook her head sadly. "No, I have no faith in Willis at all. I'll never believe in him again. But that isn't his type of thing. He might hint to someone that I could be found watching the construction at a certain time but he wouldn't admit to himself why he was doing it. To run me down deliberately — no, not Willis."

"But you aren't safe, are you?" Melody persisted. "After all, I heard Willis tell you that you are in danger. He was really frightened for you."

"Poor Willis," Randi said in a tone of such pity that Melody knew her love for him had gone completely. There was only pity for his inadequacy as a man. "But there is nothing to worry about." Randi tried to sound confident. "Mr. Lancing will bring me back and forth. That's what he telephoned about last night. And when I'm married it will be too late to do anything. There would be no point in it."

"When you are married," Melody repeated. She looked at the big diamond that flashed on Randi's finger. "Oh, darling, I wish you would reconsider."

"It's too late now," Randi told her. "Jonas deserves a chance and I'm going to see that he gets it. Honestly, Melody, would you withdraw simply for the sake of your own safety when someone's life was at stake?"

After a long pause Melody said, "No, of course not."

Randi smiled. "When you meet him you'll like him. You can't help liking him. You'll see why he is worth it. And you're to live there after we are married."

"But why must you go back today," Melody asked, "if you are to be married so soon? Surely you can't go on working on the book at this point."

"No, not on the book, but there are plans to make for the wedding and changes in the house. I'm to be married there, you know. That's the way Jonas wants it."

"At least, will you let me decorate the altar for you?

You know, we always planned to do that for each other when we married."

Randi nodded and summoned up a smile. "Of course. Why, it wouldn't be legal if you didn't help. I got you the loveliest bridesmaid's dress. Fortunately we are the same size. I can't wait to see you in it."

The doorbell rang and she heard Andy's shrill voice call eagerly, "Melody? It's me, Melody. I'm here."

It was Melody who admitted him and smiled at John Lancing. "I understand that my sister has acquired a bodyguard."

"I'll bring her back alive," Lancing promised. He turned to Randi. "Sorry to be late. I had a sort of idea about keeping Mr. King safe and I was checking this morning to see how it works out."

"What kind of a sort of idea?"

He shook his head smiling. "This will work only if it's a dead secret. Shall we be on our way?" He waved to Melody. "I'll pick up my urchin this afternoon. See you then."

As Randi fell into step beside him he said, "I hear from Cary that was rather a close shave you had last evening on your way back from New York."

She shivered. "This thing is becoming a regular nightmare. All my life I've lived in such a safe world; and now it seems to be strewn with dangers and — and booby traps."

"There's only a short time left now," he reminded her. "After that there would be nothing to gain by hurting you."

The DANGER sign was back on the sidewalk under the scaffolding and men were at work on the building, but today, with John's hand firmly on her arm, Randi was steered rapidly away from it without pausing to watch the work going on. At the corner she found herself, from habit, looking down the street toward Willis's office but there was no sign of him. She wondered if he knew about Hubert King's attempt to kill her by wrecking the car the day before.

On Jonas King's doorstep John waited until the butler had opened the door and then, with a gay wave of the hand and a cheery "Keep your chin up," he ran lightly along the path toward the guesthouse.

"There's someone with Mr. King," Luther told her, "but he said for you to go right up to the library."

"Mr. Hubert?" she asked in a scared whisper.

"Mr. Hubert doesn't get in this house," Luther said grimly. "Those are Mr. King's strict orders. No, this is a stranger, a young man named Peters."

The library door was open and Jonas looked up from his desk to smile at Randi. "Come in, my dear."

The young man seated beside the desk rose and turned to face the girl. He was about twenty-five, with an open, freckled face, sandy hair, and observant eyes. He held himself with an erect, almost military, precision.

"This is Mr. Peters, who has applied for the job you are leaving vacant." Jonas's expression was rather odd; he was watching the young man intently. "My fiancée, Miss Scott."

Randi held out her hand with the simple friendliness that was characteristic of her. The young man took it in his, giving her an unexpectedly shrewd look. He would remember everything about her, she realized.

"I think you will enjoy the job," she told him.

"I am sure I will. I can't wait to get started. The book sounds well worth doing."

"Then," Jonas said, "we will call it settled. Tomorrow about ten Miss Scott will show you what she has been doing and put you in the picture so you will be able to carry on. I won't be working on the book immediately but I will put you on the payroll at once." He smiled. "It isn't easy to get trained assistants in a village. I feel singularly fortunate to have you come." Again there was an odd expression on his face.

The young man was aware of it but appeared to ignore Jonas's attitude. "I feel grateful to get a job that supplies living quarters and meals as well as salary. If you are sure you aren't going to need me today, I'll just clear out of my room in the village and get ready to settle in the one you have for me here. Thank you and good day, sir. Good morning, Miss Scott."

Jonas waited until he had gone and then he came to kiss Randi's cheek lightly.

"Well, you didn't waste any time in finding a new secretary!" she exclaimed in surprise.

He nodded. "I am very much interested in young Mr. Peters. It seems that brother Hubert suggested that he apply for the job."

"Oh, no, Jonas!" Randi cried in horror. "You mustn't do that. It's too much of a risk."

He smiled. "Don't worry, my dear. It's going to be quite all right — and very interesting. And I shall be on my guard."

"But to let him live here? Surely that isn't necessary."

"Staying here was really his idea. He was willing to take a much lower salary for the sake of getting room and board. As a matter of fact, he was greatly disappointed when I said he couldn't move in until tomorrow. He seemed to be — uh — primed for action."

Jonas forestalled further protests on her part. "Did you get the rings?"

She nodded and extended her left hand rather shyly. He took it in his own and looked at the blazing diamond.

"There is an old saying: 'Wear it in health.' Wear this in health and happiness, my dear. How did you manage to get back so early this morning? You must have started about seven. I didn't intend you to do that. I hope they made you comfortable at the Plaza."

"Oh, we didn't stay in New York," Randi said carelessly. "After the shopping — and I think you will like the things I chose — I only hope I wasn't too extravagant — I was tired so we just drove back home."

Her voice trailed off. Jonas's eyes swept over her telltale face. So that was it! Not only Cary but Randi had fallen in love. There was understanding and tenderness and compassion in his face. So that was why they had not risked spending an evening together. You see, Billings, he said mentally to his lawyer, there are people who are completely trustworthy, capable of any amount of disinterested goodness. Sometimes it pays to remember that.

Because Jonas made no audible comment about her unexpected return, Randi went on rather uneasily, "If you are going to have someone else do your secretarial work, how am I to fill in my time from now on?"

"I thought," he said casually, "you might help Cary now and then. I've been arranging for him to make some talks in the local schools."

"Oh, no, I —"

He smiled faintly. "And, of course, you'll have to consult with the housekeeper. She is under your orders now. You are to have free scope in altering anything to suit you, whether it is furniture or the household routine, or the staff itself. I understand Mrs. Wilkes hopes to find a suitable personal maid for you. Apparently someone showed up this morning to apply for the job. I told Mrs. Wilkes you would see the girl at your convenience."

"Of course," Randi said quietly, acquiescing to Jonas's ideas. Only her heart rebelled. She could not work with Cary, day after day. She must not see him at all. And she remembered, with a pang, Alice Meynell's heartbreaking sonnet beginning, "I must not think of thee." She found herself trying to thrust away the words of that sonnet, of the pain of the woman who forced herself all day long to shun the thought of the man she loved, but who had no such control over her dreams, so that, as soon as she slept, "I run, I run, I am gathered to thy heart."

Love with honor, she told herself firmly. I am going to protect Jonas; I am going to honor his trust in me. Forever.

ii

"I don't know what to say, Miss Scott," Mrs. Wilkes admitted. "The girl seems perfectly satisfactory; her references *look* all right —"

"Look all right?" Randi echoed.

"Well, yes. Unimpeachable. The only difficulty is that all three of her former employers are abroad at the moment and there is no way of checking on them. On the other hand, it isn't easy to get a personal maid here. We have to send to the city and city girls don't, as a rule, like living in a village. Not enough amusement in their time off. Not so much choice of boy friends. So we are lucky to get anyone at all."

"Let's see her," Randi suggested.

"Very well, Miss Scott." The housekeeper nodded and went out of the small informal living room on the first floor where Randi had been talking to her. A few minutes later she returned with a young girl with a mildly pretty face and vulnerable eyes, and ominously weak around the chin. "This is Sally Murton."

"How do you do, Sally," Randi said pleasantly.

The girl nodded. "All right, ma'am." Her hands clenched and unclenched, clenched and unclenched, while she stared at Randi.

"Sit down, won't you?"

The girl perched uneasily on the edge of a chair,

looking at Mrs. Wilkes in a manner that was half frightened, half defiant. She would be unlikely to talk in the older woman's presence. Randi nodded dismissal to the housekeeper, who went out. The girl expelled a quick breath of relief and relaxed for the first time.

Randi looked at her in surprise. "You aren't afraid of Mrs. Wilkes, are you? I think you will find that she is considerate and kind to work for."

"I know her kind," the girl said. "Watching you every single minute. There was a matr —" She broke off abruptly.

Randi did not appear to notice. "Who told you that I might need a maid?" she asked casually.

The girl blinked at her. "It was just chance," she said. "I was in the department store and I overheard someone in the next aisle talking about you getting married and how you would need a maid. I thought I might as well apply."

She wasn't much of a liar, Randi thought. She probably wasn't much of a maid either. It was too much coincidence that young Peters and the girl Sally should both apply on the same morning for jobs about which no one was supposed to know anything. There had been no announcement of her engagement. The information had trickled out through one of the staff or, of course, Miss Bertram.

For reasons of his own Jonas had decided to hire Peters and to keep an eye on him. Randi looked thoughtfully at the girl, at the frightened eyes with their unspoken appeal, and made up her mind.

"Suppose we try it, Sally. I shan't need much of your time until I am married, but meantime you can help Mrs. Wilkes in any way she suggests. All right?"

The girl hesitated, those telltale hands clenching, unclenching. "All right." She added belatedly, "Ma'am."

When Mrs. Wilkes had returned in response to Randi's ring, the latter said, "I am going to try Sally for a couple of weeks. For the next few days she'll be at leisure so she may be of use to you."

Mrs. Wilkes nodded. "Very well, Miss Scott. I suppose you'll want her to have a room here. Unless you have other instructions for her, I'll put Sally to work polishing the brass in the drawing room. Mr. King says the wedding will be held there."

Randi nodded. "We'll see what can be done to prepare the room. There will be no guests, you know. It is to be strictly private, but still —"

"There is an excellent man in Hartford who can decorate the room beautifully," Mrs. Wilkes suggested. "Mr. King usually calls on him when he entertains on a large scale."

"We may need his help. But my sister would like to plan and arrange it herself."

"Of course, Miss Scott. I'll just settle Sally in her room and provide her with a uniform, and I'll join you later."

That day lunch was served in the dining room. Jonas smiled at Randi. "From now on you are to take your proper place at the head of the table. What have you been doing with yourself this morning?"

"Planning changes in the blue suite, which I'd like to occupy as my own rooms. I want to get rid of those dark draperies and some of that heavy furniture and make the rooms light and bright and gay."

"Good!" He was genuinely pleased. "I told you that you would bring sunshine with you. After lunch let's take a look at what you are planning to do."

Randi led him triumphantly through the blue suite, explaining the alterations she had in mind. "Nothing drastic, you know, just letting in the light and abolishing the heavy things."

"And after that," he suggested, "you can start on the rest of the house and abolish the shadows. I knew you would be good for me. Good for us all."

As they paused in the doorway to the big drawing room he saw the girl busy polishing brass. "Who is that?"

"That is Sally Murton, the new maid Mrs. Wilkes has hired to look after me and my wardrobe." Randi laughed. "So far there is nothing to look after so she is polishing brass, helping prepare for" — there was a slight catch in her breath — "the wedding."

There were voices in the hall, and Luther spoke from the doorway. "Mr. Hamilton."

"Come in, Cary," Jonas called.

The tall young man halted as he caught sight of Randi and then he advanced slowly into the room. "I won't keep you," he said. "I just came to deliver this." He held out the small box containing the wedding ring.

Jonas opened it, nodded his approval, and handed it

back. "If you are going to be my best man you had better keep this for me."

Cary pocketed the ring without a word.

"By the way," Jonas said, "I hope you won't feel that I am imposing on your good nature, but yesterday I had a talk with a couple of local people — quite a busy day I had while you were in New York — the head of the school board, the newspaper owner, a few others. They would like you to give some informal talks in the schools this month and try to counteract the propaganda that is going on. I more or less pledged that you would do it."

"Well, I — sorry, sir, I'm afraid that is out. I have some obligations of my own coming up sooner than I expected. I was going to tell you that I'd have to leave for California in a week or two at the latest."

California, Randi thought, her heart sinking. The other side of the continent. But he was right, of course. She would not have stopped him if she could.

"I'm sorry too," Jonas said. "It's my belief that you are needed here, Cary. The time to stop trouble is when it starts, not after it has begun to snowball. Give an idea a chance to register without challenge, and it may be too late to change it."

"That is true," Cary admitted.

"Then you will think it over?"

After a pause Cary said quietly, "Yes, I'll think it over."

XII

AGAIN John Lancing walked beside Randi when she started back to the cottage. "I hear there are a couple of new employees around today," he said casually.

"Yes, a maid for me and a secretary for Jonas. And I don't — Mr. Lancing, did Cary tell you what this business is all about?"

"Yes, he told me, and my name, by the way, is John."

"Then, John, you know what Hubert King is trying to accomplish?"

"That is why I am sticking to you like a leech, my girl." He spoke lightly but his eyes were serious.

"Jonas says this secretary, this new young man Peters, heard of the job possibility through his brother Hubert."

"Well, well." John seemed more amused than perturbed.

"You don't seem to realize," Randi said sharply, "how dangerous, how risky it is to let a stranger come so near Jonas, particularly one who comes from Hubert. He might — do anything. And he offered to take a lower salary if he could live right there in the same house. I don't like it a single bit."

"Let's wait and see," John said so calmly that she looked at him in surprise. "What about the maid?"

"There's something wrong there, too," Randi said. "She was lying when she told me she overheard some-one in the department store speak of the job. I didn't even know myself that Jonas thought I should have a personal maid. And she arrived with three letters of recommendation, all from people who are out of the country and can't be checked on."

"Well!" This time John was definitely interested and somewhat disturbed.

"And that's not all. She acted afraid of Mrs. Wilkes, the housekeeper, and she said she had known a matr — and stopped as though she were giving herself away."

"Matr — matron?" John was thoughtful. "In an orphanage, perhaps? A police matron? Heaven knows. I am decidedly interested in your new maid, Randi. All right if I call you Randi?"

"Of course."

"Why did you decide to hire her instead of getting rid of her at once, if you don't believe her story?"

Randi hesitated. "Because I was so sorry for her. I don't think she has ever known any kindness, John. She is afraid of everything and everybody. She looked so appealing and yet without hope that I couldn't bear to send her away."

"It didn't occur to you, my trusting little friend, that she might be making a big play for your sympathy?"

"Perhaps she was," Randi admitted, "but she is such a poor liar that I don't think she could mislead anyone."

John laughed outright. "Watch your step, just the same." He added casually, "I wonder what Andy has been learning today. Your sister is a wonder; she is already getting results in her handling of him, teaching him not to scream for what he wants."

"I thought she would. She loves children but she doesn't overindulge them."

"Andy loves her," John said. "I should think anyone — that is, I can't understand why she hasn't married. Anyone so beautiful —"

"I hope she will some day," Randi said gently. "Of course a lot of men have wanted to marry her, ever since she was seventeen, but she would never settle for second best and there has never been anyone she really fell in love with. Then, of course, for the last few years she hasn't been very strong."

"But she could be all right in the proper climate and under the proper conditions," John said.

Randi looked at him quickly, her eyes widening in surprise. "Yes, of course she could."

"I don't suppose she — well," John cleared his throat, "here we are." He stood back to let Randi precede him into the cottage without the slightest suspicion that he had betrayed his feelings to her.

Randi smiled to herself in delight, thinking how wonderful it would be if Melody were to love this man who obviously loved her. Then she could build the rich life she so deserved, because John, with his combination of strength and gentleness, would be able to give her a life whose interests she could share with all her heart.

Andy, busy pouring colored sand from one container to another, looked up happily and went back to his pouring, utterly absorbed.

"Melody?" Randi called.

"In the kitchen," Melody called back. "I'm making a pot roast. I'm getting dinner tonight. I sent Mrs. Echo home."

Randi, about to protest, took one look at her sister's glowing cheeks, her bright eyes, and was silent. Jonas had been right.

John Lancing stood devouring Melody with his eyes. He lingered at the kitchen door and sniffed loudly. "My," he said in a pathetic tone, "it smells delicious. What a hungry man could do to that."

Melody gave him an amused look, covered the pot roast, and opened the oven. "Out of the way," she ordered. "I don't want this cake to fall."

"Not chocolate cake." He sounded wistful. "Not a real home-baked chocolate cake."

Melody could not hold back her laughter. "It's a chocolate cake," she admitted.

"Are you sure you don't need someone to help you eat all that stuff?"

The kitchen rang with Melody's laughter. "You win," she declared. "I'll set two more places, one for you and one for Andy. But this is not to be a precedent,

Mr. Lancing." She tried without success to look and sound severe. "Scandalous behavior. What kind of training is that for your son?"

"The very best," he assured her gravely. "I would hate to think of my little boy growing up helpless in a cruel world, being hungry and not knowing how to con a meal from a hardhearted woman. That's just self-preservation."

"What on earth are you doing?" Melody asked in surprise.

He had unhooked an apron from behind the door and was tying it around his waist. "I'm not the kind of man who doesn't pay for his supper," he said virtuously. "I'm going to clean up the mixing bowl and the rest of the litter in the sink."

Smiling, Randi went up to her room to change her clothes and brush her hair. Light from the setting sun poured in her window. Lights from the kitchen spilled out onto the garden, and she could hear Melody's light laugh, John's deeper voice, and Andy's shrill chatter. A family. A happy family. Tonight Melody's future seemed brighter, fuller, than it ever had before, and Randi was glad with all her heart. But she was human too. While she rejoiced for her sister, she was aware of a pang of envy when she twisted the ring with its big diamond on her hand, thinking of Cary, his fine head bowed in troubled thought when Jonas had urged him to stay, when she knew that the two of them must take separate paths.

Melody's pot roast proved to be a great success and dinner was gay. Afterwards, John firmly took over the job of washing the dishes; Melody sat down companionably in the kitchen with him while she read a bedtime story to Andy.

Randi drifted into the little living room, aware that she would be an intruder in the kitchen, switched on the television set, stared unseeingly at the screen, switched it off again, and went up to her room for a heavy sweater coat. She let herself out quietly and went around the little cottage to the small garden in the back, where she paced up and down the dark path, drawing in deep breaths of cool air.

A shadow moved and she started in alarm. It seemed as though the tree trunk had broken in two. Then someone who had been leaning against the tree was coming toward her. Before she could utter a cry, a familiar voice, pitched low, said, "Wait, Randi! I've got to talk to you."

"Willis! What are you doing here?"

"I can't let you do it, Randi. I can't let you marry King whom you don't love just because you misunderstood — because you got the wrong idea about — that woman you saw in my office."

His arms were around her now. She pushed him away from her with unexpected force.

"Don't touch me again!" Her voice shook with her anger.

"Randi!" He was genuinely surprised at her attitude. He seemed to feel injured by it, as though she were doing him an injustice. "You love me. For two years you've loved me. You can't forget that now."

"That's over, Willis. Now go away."

"You can't mean it." He caught her to him again.

This time she did not struggle. She said, her voice low and even, "I warn you, Willis, that if you kiss me I'll scream. John Lancing is in the house."

"So you're engaged to marry Jonas King but you're playing around with this — what do you call him? — Lancing? How many men do you want at one time?"

Unexpectedly her hand cracked across his face and he stumbled backward in surprise. "Now go," she said, "and don't come back. Ever."

"You don't mean it. You're mine. You're mine. Don't wait until it is too late to find that out."

"How conceited you are!"

He drew in his breath with a rasping sound. "You don't mean that. Come away with me now, Randi. We'll go away, to some place where we can be married right away."

"You must be out of your mind. I have no love left for you, Willis. No faith in you. No respect for you. Is that enough to prove that I mean what I say?"

He seized her, half in anger, half in outraged vanity.

"John!" she called.

The back door was flung open and Lancing stood in the light, a big apron tied around him, a dishtowel in his hand. He should have looked ridiculous; instead, he looked what he was at that moment, a dangerous adversary.

"Randi," he shouted, "are you all right?"

There was a stifled curse, the sound of running feet; a car door slammed, a motor raced.

Slowly Randi walked into the kitchen. Melody set a wide-eyed Andy on his feet and ran to her.

"What happened?"

"That was Willis," Randi said breathlessly, "making his last bid."

"But how did he dare come back?" Melody asked in surprise. "What did he expect to get out of it?"

"He thought he could change my mind about marrying Jonas."

John Lancing untied the apron and hung it up. Through the kitchen window above the sink he had watched that meeting, he had seen Randi in the man's arms. He wondered why she had been willing to wait so long before she called for help.

ii

"So there goes my last chance at fifty thousand dollars," Willis grunted after the Volkswagen had shot away from the cottage.

"You didn't really expect that she would leave with you tonight to get married or you wouldn't have brought me along," the woman beside him said.

"No, of course I didn't expect that. But I thought — she's been in love with me a long time. She might at least change her mind about King."

"Did you really intend to marry her if she agreed to break her engagement to King?"

"Why, yes, of course." Willis sounded genuinely surprised. "It's the only possible way to prevent that marriage that I can think of. Frankly I never dreamed of Randi wanting to marry anyone else, no matter how rich he was. I thought she was so crazy about me that she'd go on waiting indefinitely."

"And what about me?" Mavis slid her hand under his arm, over his hand on the wheel, the big emerald catching fire from a passing street light. "What plans did you have about me, darling?"

When he made no reply she laughed softly. "Perhaps you thought I'd wait patiently like that little dope until you collected that fifty thousand and became — shall we say, a widower?"

Willis drew in his breath with a gasp.

She laughed again. "How you do hate to put things into words, to face them as they are. Anyhow, that seems to have been your last bid. Now, I guess, it's up to me."

iii

Next morning Randi found Lancing silent company when they walked from her cottage to the King mansion. Now and then she was aware that he stole quick questioning looks at her, but he did not indulge in his usual gay nonsense, his lighthearted banter which had made her hope that Andy would inherit his father's sunny nature. The warm friendship he had shown her from the beginning, and that had been intensified after he met Melody, was tempered by what might almost be distrust. Somehow the walk between the two houses had never seemed so long as it did this morning, or so uncomfortable. Several times Randi tried to start a conversation, but she was given no assistance by her taciturn companion and the subject dropped.

Once more he waited at her side until the butler opened the door, then he nodded without smiling and strolled toward the guesthouse, deep in thought.

"Some packages were delivered for you this morning, Miss Scott," Luther told her. "Mr. King asked me to have them taken to the blue suite."

"Thank you. Will you send Sally to me, please."

The blue sofa in the little sitting room was cluttered with suit boxes, hatboxes, shoe boxes. On a table was the package from Tiffany's containing the diamond bracelet. Randi had forgotten how magnificent it was. Indeed, she had been so disturbed at the time she selected it at the idea of having so expensive a gift that she had barely examined it. Now she fastened it on her wrist and turned it around and around, with a woman's normal delight in its beauty. She was still looking at it, entranced, when Sally came in.

"You wanted me, ma'am? Oh, oh! How beautiful!"

"Isn't it? Will you unpack these boxes, Sally, and, before you put the clothes away, help me try them on."

One by one, while Sally exclaimed in delight, Randi tried on the dresses with the maid's help, and went down the hall to the library to display them to a smiling Jonas, walking back and forth, turning like a model.

"I've never been privileged to enjoy a private fashion show before," he said. "I'm going to have a most beautiful wife, my dear."

Randi held out her hand on which she had clasped

the diamond bracelet. "It's the most wonderful gift I've ever had. But it does make me nervous to be wearing it. Can't you keep it for me? There must be a safe in the house."

"Of course," he agreed, but when she started to slip off the glittering jewel with a sensation of relief, he checked her. "I'll take care of it tonight and put it safely away. But do wear it today to please me."

She summoned up a smile and refastened the bracelet, her fingers fumbling uncertainly.

"May I?" asked the new secretary who had come quietly into the library. He secured the bracelet quickly and competently. "That's a beautiful thing." He looked at Jonas, smiling. "The groom's gift to the bride?"

"That's right."

While Sally hung dresses on scented hangers, treed shoes, and arranged gloves and filmy hose in drawers, Randi, in the library, explained to Peters about the filing system she had worked out, showed him her research notes, the copies of the script, and described the usual method of work. All the time she kept studying him in perplexity. There was something disturbingly familiar about the nondescript-looking young man. She felt almost sure that she had seen him somewhere before, seen him under unpleasant circumstances, and yet she could not place him. She shook her head impatiently. It was like trying to remember a name. As a rule, the moment she stopped straining to recapture the memory, the name came back of its own accord. It would be so with Peters, she felt sure. Sooner or later, she would remember where she had seen him.

"Mr. King was fortunate to find someone in the village who is free to work with him and able to do the research," she said at last.

"I feel that I am fortunate in getting the job," Peters replied. "Lucky for me that I took up typing and shorthand to fill in time while I was in the Veterans Hospital."

Randi looked at him quickly. "You were in the service?"

He seemed chagrined, as though he had revealed something he had not intended to. "Vietnam. Two years."

"Were you badly wounded?" she asked.

"I'm fully recovered now." Obviously he did not want to discuss the matter further.

"What had you planned to do before your military duty interfered?" Randi asked in her friendly way. "I suppose you were training for something."

He started to answer her and then changed his mind. "I hadn't really decided." He spoke lightly, but she knew that he was not telling her the truth. In any case, she had no right to probe into his personal affairs. He got to his feet.

"Then I think the whole situation is clear in my mind. I understand," and he did not seem pleased, "that the room here will not be ready for me today, but I'll be here early tomorrow morning so I can get settled. This afternoon I'll read Mr. King's script as far as he has gone, and then I'll have the background and be more intelligent about the work. If you have no further need for me today —"

However willing, even insistent, he appeared to be to settle immediately into the King house, it was apparent that he was eager to get away from Randi and her questions.

"No, that's all, Mr. Peters." Impulsively Randi held out her hand. "Good luck to the book."

"Thank you for your good wishes, Miss Scott."

Randi heard him go down the stairs and let himself out. On impulse, she went to a window. She saw the new secretary come out of the house, go down the flagged terrace and then, instead of following the driveway to the great wall and the street beyond, he turned and went in the other direction. As she watched, perplexed, he stepped quickly off the flagged walk and onto the lawn that was just turning green, and moved forward quietly, almost furtively. Then, while she watched, he went out of sight.

XIII

THERE was a sibilant sound of whispering, and a dark shadow moved behind a clump of bushes. Peters crept forward without making any noise, his footsteps muffled by the soft ground on which he trod as lightly as a cat. Anyone watching his movements now would have been aware that this man was adept at spying.

Now there was no sound but the muffled sobs of a woman.

"Stop it," a voice said, low-pitched but angry. "Stop making a fool of yourself. Someone is going to wonder what you've been crying about. Stop it, I tell you."

"I — I c-can't help it," said a younger, higher-pitched voice.

"Of course you can help it. I want you to get back to the house now. You understand what you have to do?"

"Y-yes."

"Remember what will happen to you if you fail," the angry voice said. "This is your one chance."

"I told you I'd do my best."

"You'll do as you are told," the voice said roughly. It was a woman's voice and now the woman moved. Peters ducked behind a clump of bushes, thankful for his dark suit. The woman was, from this distance at least, beautiful.

"All right." It was a despairing, defeated whisper.

The woman came closer, tall and blond, with a lush figure, full red lips, hot angry eyes. She raised her hand to straighten her hair and a large emerald flashed on her finger. Then she went past Peters, around the side of the house, and, after a quick searching glance at the windows, down the driveway toward the street.

Peters remained unmoving. He heard the muffled sobs go on. Then the girl obviously tried to get herself under control, to check her tears. He heard her blow her nose, and then saw the dark shadow move, a slim girl in a black uniform with a trim white organdy apron and a frilled cap. As she came toward him he stepped out from behind the bushes. The girl started back and gave a frightened little scream which she attempted to stifle. Her eyes were red and swollen from crying. Worse than that, they were frankly terrified.

"Don't be afraid," Peters said gently. "Please don't be afraid."

The girl looked at him uneasily, her head moving from side to side like a wild animal scenting danger.

"I'm not going to hurt you, you know." Peters's voice was gentle, hypnotic. "Not going to hurt you. Not going to hurt you."

He had caught her attention, but she still looked as though she would run away at a moment's notice if he took so much as a quick step toward her. Carefully he refrained from moving.

"No one is going to be allowed to hurt you," he said,

and this time she really looked at him. This time she did not believe him.

"Yes, they will, unless I do what they tell me."

"Has anyone hurt you?" he asked, still in that gentle voice.

Unexpectedly she laughed, a bitter, disillusioned laugh. "People always hurt you when you don't do what they want," she said scornfully. "You know that."

"I won't hurt you." Moving cautiously so as not to terrify the girl, Peters stretched out his hand, touched her cold one lightly. "I won't hurt you." Now he had got her attention, her eyes met his. She watched him, half distrustfully, half believing. His fingers closed around her hand, but so lightly that she would know she could pull away at the slightest touch. "Perhaps I can help you. That's what friends are for, you know."

"You aren't a friend of mine."

"But I'd like to be," he told her. "My name is Henry Peters. My friends call me Hal." He waited but she made no comment. "What's your name?"

"Sally," she said. "Sally Murton."

"Do you work here, Sally?"

"I've — just started. I'm to be Mrs. King's maid."

"Mrs. King? Oh, yes, you mean Miss Scott."

"She's awfully pretty, isn't she?" the girl said wistfully.

"Very pretty," he agreed. "How did you find out about this job, Sally?"

Her mouth closed stubbornly and he was wise enough to drop the subject.

"When is your time off?"

"I don't know yet."

"How about going to the movies with me on your first free night?"

She looked at him as though seeking some kind of trap, and he wondered what sort of past the girl had had that made her believe the whole world to be her enemy.

"I'd really like to take you," he said again. "I don't know many people here and it gets lonely at times. It's nice to have someone to talk to. Especially when the someone is a pretty girl." Here —" He pulled out a notebook and scrawled something, tore out the page and handed it to her. "This is my telephone number just in case you should get tonight off. After that I'll be living here too, so we'll see each other a lot. At least, I hope we will."

"All right," she said, unexpectedly shy. "I guess maybe I could." She slipped the paper into her pocket, gave him a tentative smile.

As he heard the whir of a power mower growing louder he said, "Then I'll be seeing you, Sally. Soon, I hope." He nodded cheerfully to her and went on around the house. Sally, bemused, did not notice that he went toward the back rather than toward the street.

She stood staring after him. He was kind. In her stormy young life she had known little kindness. *I won't hurt you,* he had said, and she had — almost — believed him. Then he had said that nobody would be allowed to hurt her. Enough to make you laugh, that was. If he knew what she knew, if he had heard what that awful woman, Miss Bertram, had been saying to her, he would know how silly it was to believe that people wouldn't hurt you if they could, if you disobeyed them. Put you in prison, that's what they could do if they wanted to. If you didn't follow orders.

It had seemed easy enough in the first place. But that was before she had met Miss Scott, who had been considerate and had tried to make things pleasant for her. She had not expected that an employer would be so friendly and sort of easy in her ways. She didn't give you orders. She asked you to do things and she said please.

Sally wondered what it would be like to change places with Miss Scott, to be beautiful and happy and about to marry a millionaire who adored her; to have beautiful clothes and a diamond bracelet; to have everything safe and wonderful. She had never, even in the most glamorous movie, seen such lovely clothes as those she had hung on scented hangers as part of Miss Scott's trousseau. Like living in a movie, it was.

Her hands clenched, unclenched. What was she going to do? Suppose she failed? Suppose she was caught? Miss Scott would never understand, never forgive her, never trust her again. And Miss Bertram would carry out her threat.

Sally thought of Mr. Peters — his friends called him Hal, he had told her — and how he had said that he would like to help her. If only she dared ask him! If only she dared tell him the truth. But she knew what would happen. He might try to be kind but he would never trust her, never want to see her. A pretty girl, that's what he had called her, and said it would be nice to have someone to talk to. But if he knew about her he would turn away in contempt and leave her to Miss Bertram.

I'd do anything, anything, Sally said fiercely to herself, to be free. Anything.

ii

The telephone rang in the guesthouse and Cary answered it. After listening for a while he said, "Of course, Mr. Billings. I'll be at your office as soon as possible, a quarter of an hour, twenty minutes at most. May I bring my friend Lancing with me? . . . A colleague who is very much involved in both situations. . . . Yes, I said both."

When he had set down the telephone he turned to Lancing, who had been typing busily at a desk until the phone rang.

"John, that was Billings, Jonas King's lawyer, the man —"

"Oh, yes, I remember."

"He's got something from the state police and it seemed better to discuss it in his office rather than here. Will you come along?"

"Of course." Lancing shoved back his chair. "I won't

need a topcoat. It must be nearly sixty today. What a wonderful spring!"

It was not until the two men were in Cary's Renault that Lancing asked, "What is it all about?"

"I don't know. It's the state police story, not mine."

"I didn't mean that. I heard you tell Billings that I am involved in both situations. What did you mean by that?"

"I meant that you were working with me as a colleague in the fight against the subversives. And I assumed, because you are definitely interested in Randi Scott's sister, that you are involved in the problem of Randi's safety. Right?"

"Right," Lancing said, but his lips tightened. He thought of Randi clasped in a man's arms in the dark garden. She had certainly taken her time about calling for help; she had been in no apparent hurry to terminate that surreptitious interview. He hoped that Cary was not mistaken in his estimate of the girl. Or — well, as they would be hopelessly divided by her marriage, it might be better if he saw her without any illusions. Then he would have fewer regrets. It was possible she was, after all, only a crafty little gold digger. One thing was sure. If any further attempt was made on Jonas King's life after the marriage, one person to profit would be Randi. Lancing wondered how much Melody knew about her sister's interest in the man Jameson, and what she thought of the engagement to Jonas King.

The lawyer's offices occupied the second floor of the bank building. There was an impressive reception room, a library with its walls lined with legal volumes, and four private offices, the largest of which was occupied by Billings himself.

The stocky lawyer came out of the reception room to greet Cary, shake hands with Lancing, and conduct them back to his office where Lieutenant Barker of the state police was waiting.

"I take it," Billings said, "that Hamilton has kept you abreast of this most disturbing situation."

Lancing nodded without speaking.

"I don't believe," the lawyer said with characteristic caution, "I know what your position is here."

"Lancing," Cary explained, "is not merely an old friend but, as I informed you, he is a colleague of mine. We are working on the same problem. At the present time he is spending six months in the East, hoping that he can find some way of pooling our finds and consolidating our efforts. As a rule, Lancing works in the Southwest, in the vicinity of Phoenix."

Billings nodded to the lieutenant, indicating that the floor was his.

"There is no question, to begin with," Barker said crisply, "about the rope which held the scaffolding. It was deliberately cut. That was no accident."

"Any trace of the man with the knife?" Cary asked.

"You remember," Lancing said, "Andy told us he saw a man with a knife just before the scaffold fell. He was the only one of us to be looking up at the time."

"Andy?" The lieutenant's voice was sharp.

Lancing grinned. "Sorry. He's not a possible witness. He is my four-year-old son."

"Too bad. Of course, we have a few conflicting accounts of the accident, the usual thing, and several people who claim they saw a man behaving in a mysterious way." The lieutenant sighed. "That always happens. According to one woman, the man must have been seven feet tall and he was armed with a curved weapon that sounded, from her description, like a beheading knife."

When Lancing laughed he said, "I don't know how much more reliable the other witnesses are. One is a man who has claimed to be a witness to every accident we have had in the past thirty years. He distinctly saw a dwarfish figure slink away from the building, looking, so far as I can make out, like Peter Lorre. In fact, he wasn't sure that it was not Peter Lorre. The third witness was a woman who rents a furnished room in one of those big houses on the Green across from the building. Too bad the way some of the old houses have been cut up. Anyhow, the house is clear across the Green and she wasn't wearing her glasses at the time. But she insists she saw him and she thinks she would recognize him a second time. All we have to do is find him. So that's that."

He saw the expression on Cary's face and added, a trifle defensively, "We can't perform miracles, you know, Mr. Hamilton."

"I don't expect miracles," Cary said, his voice hard.

"But I did hope you would carry out your promise to keep an eye on Hubert King and his colleagues, or associates, or henchmen, or whomever he is dealing with."

"We don't have unlimited manpower." The lieutenant was angry now, resentful of the implied criticism in Cary's words. "It wasn't until this morning that we were able to get some men free to assign to the job, one to watch King and the others to follow anyone who seems to be working with him."

"You're a bit late," Cary told him. "You might have been disastrously late."

"Well, we won't let Hubert out of sight again," the lieutenant promised him. "But what I really want, Mr. Hamilton, is to get the names of any possible associates. We don't want to waste manpower if we can avoid it; on the other hand, we can't afford to pass up any bets. We have assigned someone to the nurse, Miss Bertram, who will pick her up today and keep an eye on her from now on. But the most important thing, and I admit I don't know where to look for it, is the missing link between Hubert King and Miss Scott. Who is the person who informed Hubert of Miss Scott's habit of stopping to watch the construction and the times at which she usually passed it?"

"I think I can answer that," John Lancing said abruptly. He was careful not to look at Cary. "Last evening, when I walked home with Miss Scott — Hamilton and I have arranged that she won't go out by herself after that business in New York — I stayed on for dinner. Afterwards I was helping her sister with the dishes and Randi went out into the garden. I heard her call out for me. There was a man with her but he got away. I know he had a car because I heard him drive off."

"A man?" Cary's hands gripped the arms of his chair. "Was she hurt? Who was it? Did you see him?"

"I saw him just vaguely. It was dark in the garden. But, according to her sister," Lancing busied himself lighting a cigarette, his attention on the process, avoiding Cary's eyes, as though giving him time to pull himself together without embarrassing witnesses, "his name is Willis Jameson. Only a day or two before, he had warned Randi she was in danger. He is the missing link; it appears that he is Hubert's lawyer. He is also the man to whom Randi Scott was engaged for two years, in fact, until the day before she agreed to marry Jonas King."

Cary stared at his friend in disbelief. Randi engaged? There had been no mention of any other man. He sat with his thoughts in a turmoil, staring at his hands. Randi! He had believed in her so completely and yet his first suspicions must have been correct. All that business of protesting over the buying of the jewelry had been so much dust in his eyes. Star dust, it was true. He had let himself be blinded, misled, because she was so lovely, so gay, so warm. She appeared to be so completely honest.

"I knew about the previous engagement," Billings said evenly. "Mr. King told me that Miss Scott had been engaged to another man." He added without expression, "And that she broke the engagement the day after Mr. King proposed to her."

After a moment the lieutenant said, "Willis Jameson, a lawyer? Oh, yes, I've seen him around town. Nicelooking fellow. The girls all fall for him, I believe. But I didn't know he was engaged; I assumed he was playing the field, though I knew he had a beautiful blonde around. I've seen them at Sands Roadhouse. Not much money. Nothing against him that I know of." He made some notes. "Anything else?"

Again it was Lancing who volunteered information. "Mr. King has acquired a new secretary who is to take over Miss Scott's duties after her marriage. A man named Peters."

"Do you know anything about him?"

Lancing grinned. "He was told about the job by Hubert King."

"For God's sake!" the lieutenant exploded. Lancing laughed and began to talk fast. Again the lieutenant made notes. "I hope you know what you are doing," he said at last. "Is that all?"

"There's a new character on the scene, a lady's maid who applied for the job yesterday. Said she overheard someone saying that Miss Scott would need a maid. References from former employers that sound fine but cannot be checked because, curiously, all of the people who are supposed to have written them are out of the country. Her name is Sally Murton. Miss Scott," and his face was expressionless, "said she was sorry for her and said the girl appeared to be afraid. To judge by what the maid let drop unintentionally, she either has come from an orphanage or she has a criminal background."

"We'll check her out at once," the lieutenant said. "I can't figure why Miss Scott is taking such a chance. But I must say one thing; if a man ever managed to get himself surrounded by beasts of prey, Mr. Jonas King seems to be the man."

XIV

"I THINK," Jonas said, "it would be a pleasant idea if you were to ask your sister to dine here tonight. It is high time we became acquainted. We'll see if we can get Cary and Lancing to join us."

Randi agreed, gave her instructions to the house-keeper rather hesitantly, as it was the first time she had done so, and then called Melody.

"I'll wear one of my trousseau dresses," she said over the telephone, "and you can change here. I got you two dresses when I got mine. I won't come home this afternoon but I'll ask John to bring you when he calls for Andy. He is invited to dinner too."

When she had put down the telephone Randi found that she did not know whether to be glad or sorry that Cary would be dining with them. She did not know which was the stronger, the delight of seeing him or the misery of knowing that they would be separated. She knew, too, that she must be guarded so that Melody, who knew her so well, would not guess that she had fallen in love with this man.

The afternoon passed slowly. Jonas had decided to rest in preparation for the evening. There was no work

to do on the book, which Peters was reading. Randi
paced up and down the formal drawing room. There
was something wrong with the man Peters. For some
reason John Lancing had not seemed to be disturbed by
the fact that he had come from Hubert King. She must
find an opportunity to tell Cary about the new secretary
and his curious behavior in sneaking around the house
as he had done. Again she was puzzled by that dim
sense of familiarity. She was positive she had seen the
man before. But where? Where?

It was after five when John Lancing brought Melody
and Andy from the cottage. Randi, who had been in the
suite that was eventually — in so short a time — to be
her own, ran down the stairs to meet her sister and
conduct her up to the front suite.

"This is to be yours," she said, "as long as you want
to live here."

Melody looked around. "Heavens, what splendor! I
had no idea the place was so — so luxurious, Randi."

"Jonas asked you to come early because he wants a
chance to get acquainted with you. He thought there
would be time to talk before dinner."

Melody looked at her sister. "Of course," she said,
trying to speak brightly, gaily. "Oh, how lovely!" She
had caught sight of a coral chiffon dinner dress with
matching slippers which Randi had spread out for her.

"It's for you. I hope it fits. Shall I send Sally to
you?"

"Sally?"

"My new maid."

"Jeepers! You really are living in the lap of luxury. No, I'll manage." Melody laughed. "As though I haven't been managing to dress myself all my life. But you can come in and zip me up if you will."

Randi went quietly along the hallway with its deep carpeting and opened the door of the sitting room in her own suite. When she had bathed in scented water in the sunken tub, a long leisurely bath, she pulled on the new yellow negligee and slippers and opened the door to the bedroom.

Sally was moving with a caution that surprised her. After putting out the evening dress Randi had selected, she went to the dressing table. Something flickered in the mirror. The girl had picked up the diamond bracelet which Randi had removed before bathing. For a long moment she hesitated and then she thrust it into her pocket and started hastily toward the door.

Randi moved then. "Sally!" She looked gravely and sorrowfully at the white-faced maid.

Sally started and uttered a half scream; one hand tightened convulsively on her pocket.

"Give it to me, Sally," Randi said. "You'll have to give it back, you know."

The girl stared at her, one hand in a fist, the other gripping her pocket. Then she drew the bracelet out of her pocket and handed it to Randi. There was an expression of utter defeat on her face. She stood swaying as though she were about to faint.

Randi clasped the bracelet on her own wrist and then she took the girl's arm. Sally made no attempt to get away; she waited listlessly. For a moment Randi wished, in a kind of exasperation, that the girl would at least try to fight for herself. She eased her onto a low slipper chair and sat down on the edge of the bed, moving aside the pale green evening dress.

"Why did you do it?" she asked at length.

Sally blinked at her as though she could not even understand her meaning. She sat sagging on the slipper chair, head down, shoulders bent forward, only those desperate hands opening and closing, opening and closing.

"Why?" Randi repeated. "You must have known that suspicion would fall on you at once if you stole it. You must have realized that you would have difficulty in disposing of it. What did you hope to gain?"

"I thought — I hoped — maybe I could get away. There is a man — a fence I guess you'd call him — in New York. At least there used to be. Once, when I was twelve, my father made me take a ring to him. He bought it. He might of bought the bracelet. It could of given me enough money to run away."

"But you can't run away," Randi said gently. "No one can solve anything by running away, Sally."

For the first time there was a flash of something like spirit in Sally's defeated eyes, like mockery in her voice. "That's what you think, Miss Scott. What do you know about it? What do people like you ever know about it? There's only one thing for people like me to do, and that is to run away. It's the only way I could ever be free." She repeated broodingly, "Free." Using a word that had no reality for her; an unattainable dream.

"Free of what?" Randi laid her hand on Sally's arm, felt it quivering, and a wave of pity went over her for this helpless and defenseless girl, this born victim. "Look here, Sally, and try to listen to me." The girl did not stir. "Look at me," she repeated more urgently.

The vague, frightened eyes met hers. Randi smiled at her as confidently as she could, attempting to give the girl some of the reassurance she so badly needed. "Sally, I want to help you, not to hurt you."

Someone else had said that, the young man named Peters. But in all her short, unhappy life no one had ever really meant it.

"Yeah?" There was disillusionment and defeat in her face.

"You're in trouble, aren't you, Sally?"

"Yeah," she repeated, as dully, as mechanically, as a sleepwalker. "I'm in trouble. Big trouble."

"But don't you see that I can't help you unless I understand clearly what the situation is, what you have become involved in?"

"How can you help me, anyhow? If it isn't Them," and she made the word sound as though it were capitalized, "it will be the police. In the long run, I guess, it was bound to be the police. No matter what I did."

"Why does it have to be the police?" Randi was still gentle, though she wanted to shake a little spirit into the girl. "Who are they, these people you seem to be so afraid of?"

There was no answer.

"Look," Randi said, and she could not altogether control her impatience with this spinelessness, "I don't want to report you to the police if I can avoid it, if there is any possible alternative. Can't you understand that? I don't think you are bad. I don't believe you even wanted to steal, you just thought you had to. But if I don't know what is wrong I can't help you; and unless I can feel justified in letting you go, I'll have to report to the police, not as a matter of punishment but because I respect law."

"You mean — maybe you wouldn't tell the police?" The words were an incredulous whisper.

"Not if it can be avoided. I don't want you to have a record. This was — just a mistake, I'm sure of that. Why won't you trust me, Sally?"

There was a long pause. Sally looked at the other girl in a kind of desperate calm. This lovely girl, kind as she appeared, would never be able to understand so she could not help her; she would not, in the long run, want to help her or save her from the police. Certainly there was no way, with the best will in the world, she could save her from Them.

"Tell me about your family," Randi said when the silence had stretched out almost beyond endurance.

Her family? Sally was bewildered. People wanted to know the silliest things. Why didn't Miss Scott come right out and say how bad she had been about the bracelet? But for some reason, it wasn't the attempted theft of the bracelet that worried her.

Her mother, Sally said, died when she was three years old. There were no other children and she had no memory of her mother. She was left in her father's care. Sometimes he had been good to her; most of the time he neglected her. Now and then, he had been downright brutal, beating her because he had suffered some unexpected disappointment and he had to take it out on someone. She did not blame him; that was the way people naturally behaved, hitting out at you if you happened to get in the way.

Then he had been involved in a robbery. She never really got the thing straight because no one ever explained and she had been very young. The whole thing, as Randi gathered from the somewhat incoherent story, had been a badly bungled piece of amateur theft, in which Sally's father, as much victim as criminal, was pulling the chestnuts out of the fire for his more astute and experienced companions. In any case, he had received as his share of the loot a ring which he had forced his twelve-year-old daughter to take to the receiver of stolen goods. He had been caught and sent to prison, where a few months later he died of pneumonia.

Sally had been placed in an orphanage. Apparently, it had not been particularly bad; but it had not been run in accordance with modern and enlightened principles. The matron had believed in strict justice rather than in justice tempered with mercy. And Sally, who as a child had lived in fear of her father, lived as a young girl in fear of the matron and all people who represented authority or justice, which, in her eyes, was a grim balancing of the scales without understanding or compassion. And now she lived in fear of Them.

She had not been pretty enough or clever enough to attract people who wanted to adopt a child; only one couple had displayed any interest in her and they had rejected her in the long run because of what they regarded as her criminal heritage. At eighteen she had been sent out to earn her living. She had been trained to do housework, but the day she was released she had encountered Mavis Bertram, who had come to the orphanage twice in the past few months, claiming that she was interested in helping to place the youngsters to their advantage when they were ready to leave.

The Bertram woman had told her of the job with Miss Scott, soon to be Mrs. Jonas King. She had told her that she must get the job and had provided her with fake references. Then she was — Sally gulped and for the first time the flow of talk stopped.

"Go on," Randi said, still gently.

"I don't know exactly," the girl said, her eyes frightened. "But after Mr. King dies of a heart attack I am to use the combination She gave me and open his safe. I'm to get his will and destroy it.

"Miss — She said," Sally went on in that dead little voice, "that if I didn't do as I was told I'd be sent to prison as my father had been because I pawned that ring he stole."

"But Sally," Randi cried out in anger, "no one could do that to you. Not possibly."

"They — couldn't?"

"Of course not. Why you were only twelve years old at the time. Just a child."

Sally raised questioning eyes. She didn't know whom to believe. She was terrified of the tall blonde woman with the angry eyes. She placed instinctive trust in this girl with the kind eyes, the gentle smile, the soft voice. But like many people who have not learned to think for themselves, she was more impressed by the power of evil than by the power of good. Her hands clenched, unclenched in indecision. What should she do? Whom should she believe?

"And so you decided to steal the bracelet and run away," Randi said.

"I saw it and I thought — if I could sell it, I could go to some other town and maybe be free to start a new way of life, and it seemed to me I'd be willing to do anything to get away."

For a long time Randi was silent while Sally watched her, half in hope, half in dread. Then she said, "Sally, I may be foolish but I want you to have another chance. Another? Perhaps the first chance you've really had. I'm not going to report to the police about the bracelet. I'm going to trust you to try faithfully to earn your living. No one here will hurt you. As for Them — they can't do anything to you, Sally." Randi's hand tightened on the girl's thin arm. "Believe me," she said earnestly, "they can't hurt you."

She broke off in dismay and distress as Sally dropped into a crumpled heap at her feet, clutching at the filmy yellow negligee, sobbing.

"If only I had known you before, known someone like you. It's too late for me now."

"It's never too late to begin over again," Randi assured her stoutly. "Now I want you to dry your tears and help me dress."

With Sally's eager if awkward and inexpert help, Randi put on the green dress, the pale green of new leaves in spring, which fell in soft folds over her bare shoulders and down to her feet, and then brushed the soft cap of dark hair until it gleamed.

"You look lovely," Sally breathed. "Just lovely. It must be wonderful to know you are beautiful."

Beautiful? Randi looked at her image in the glass, wondering if it were true. She was much too pale. The shock of Sally's confession — and she was aware that Sally herself was ignorant of the implications of what she had said — had driven the blood away from her heart. After Jonas had died of a heart attack, Sally was to rob his safe. *After a heart attack.* So something had been planned, something that was to happen within the next few days.

She applied lipstick lavishly to her white lips and summoned up a smile. Well, that was better. She looked more like herself. It was a braver face that looked back at her.

"Take the evening off and have fun," she suggested. "I won't want you again tonight because I'll be going home with my sister after dinner." She paused in the doorway. "Do you have any friends here?"

Sally hesitated, and then she returned Randi's smile

radiantly. "Yes, ma'am," she said with unexpected confidence, "I do have a friend."

"Good. Then good night, Sally."

"Good night, ma'am. And thank you. Oh, thank you!"

Sally listened to Randi's high heels as she went swiftly down the hall to the front suite. Then she picked up the telephone in the bedroom. She dialed a number and listened, her heart beating harder.

A man's voice said in a businesslike way, "Peters speaking."

"This," she said shyly, "is Sally."

ii

Melody turned away from the mirror in the front guest suite to answer her sister's knock on the door.

"How lovely you look, Randi!" she exclaimed.

Randi smiled at her. "So do you. You need bright colors. Tonight you are going to capture whatever is left of John Lancing's heart that is not already yours."

"I?" Melody's dark-fringed eyes gazed at her in genuine surprise.

Randi laughed. "Don't tell me," she said teasingly, "you haven't seen the symptoms. You've had enough men in love with you to recognize them. He fell for you like a ton of bricks. One look. That's all that was necessary."

Color deepened in Melody's cheeks. "That is absurd."

"If you really think so," Randi said, as she zipped up the coral-colored dress for her sister, "watch your step and don't encourage him, because he is in earnest. Very much so. He doesn't like me but he thinks you are wonderful."

"Doesn't like you!" Melody exclaimed indignantly.

"Hey," Randi laughed, "there's no rule that a man has to love a girl's family if he loves her."

"But why shouldn't he like you?"

"I don't know. It was only when — it was after Willis came to the house that he changed toward me."

"Randi! That bracelet! It's the most magnificent thing I ever saw. Is that from Mr. King?"

"Of course. Now come down and meet him. You're going to like him, Melody. He's a rather wonderful person."

Jonas King was waiting in the big drawing room, now a blaze of light and filled with flowers. Randi had not realized before how impressive he was. Dinner clothes were becoming to his spare figure. Some men looked like penguins in a dinner jacket, but not Jonas King. He came to the door to welcome the two girls, smiling with pleasure at the glowing picture they made.

Watching Melody rather anxiously, Randi saw with pleasure that she recognized Jonas's quality at once, both his fineness and his basic kindness and integrity. She had not doubted for a moment Jonas's liking Melody. He wouldn't be able to resist her.

"So you are Melody." He took her hand in both of his, smiling down at the exquisite face. "No wonder —"

He broke off to say to Randi, "Would you mind very much letting us get acquainted by ourselves?"

"Of course not," Randi said readily if a trifle blankly, and she wandered out of the room and into the smaller living room at the back of the house.

"No wonder what?" Melody asked when her sister had gone.

"No wonder Randi believes you are — uh — a very special person." He drew up a chair beside her.

"She thinks you are special too," Melody assured him.

"But you are worried about your sister, aren't you?"

Melody responded to the candor in his eyes. "I want her to be happy, Mr. King." Seeing his expression, she corrected herself quickly. "Jonas. Naturally I am somewhat worried about this marriage because of the difference in your ages and all that. I've always believed that marriage should be —" Her voice trailed off.

"Randi isn't going to be unhappy," he told her in his quiet voice. "She is going to be taken care of. Eventually she will find happiness. I think I can almost promise you that, if any person can promise happiness for another. I will risk making a prediction, if you like. Randi will make her life full and rich and rewarding; she will leave behind her a better world than she found because she is a giver rather than a receiver. But sooner or later, she will receive. She will find all the fulfillment of a happy wife and mother."

He excused himself and went out of the room. When he returned he found her looking at a great vase of

American beauty roses. "This," and he handed her a letter, "is for your keeping."

Melody looked down in surprise at the envelope marked *Randi*. She turned to him, a question in her wide dark-blue eyes, which gave her that special quality of beauty.

"I want you to keep this, Melody," Jonas said. "Some day you are going to give it to Randi, some day when I can no longer speak for myself. Until then, I trust it to your safekeeping. It will, I think, explain why she has been put in a position that must seem to you to be unnecessarily difficult; perhaps even painful."

Melody nodded and opened her evening bag. She thrust the envelope into it. "I'll keep it for her," she promised. "Somehow I feel, as Randi does, that you would ask nothing that it was not right to ask."

Jonas took her slender hand in his. "Thank you," he said quietly. Then he raised his head and turned. "I think our guests have arrived. You have met Cary Hamilton, haven't you? And John Lancing?"

When Randi returned to the drawing room it was to find an apparently lighthearted party awaiting. She saw with relief that Melody and Jonas had established a friendly relationship, though she had been almost prepared to wager that they would. No one could resist Melody's loveliness, and she knew Melody was intelligent enough to see Jonas's fine qualities. But they seemed to be even better friends than she had dared to hope.

Lancing drew Melody away on the pretext of con-

sulting her about Andy, and Randi found herself between Cary and Jonas, both of whom were endeavoring
to keep the conversation impersonal and gay.

Dinner, at which Randi took her place as hostess at
Jonas's request, was delicious and perfectly served by
the unobtrusive butler and a waitress. Once when Lancing and Cary were bantering, Randi found herself
twisting the diamond bracelet and thinking about Sally.
Had she done the right thing? Should she have reported the girl's attempt at theft? Was she encouraging
crime? It was difficult to know what was right to do.
She sighed. She would have to talk to Cary about it, to
find out what was best to be done. Anyhow, he must be
told about the girl's association with Mavis Bertram
and the former nurse's threat of prison, her blackmail
attempt in order to make sure that Jonas King's will
was stolen.

After a heart attack. After his death. Something
must be done at once about this immediate threat. But
what could be done without alarming Jonas and there-
fore endangering him?

A moment's pause in the gay chatter made her look
up suddenly, snapping out of her absorption in her own
thoughts to see Cary's eyes resting on her face, John
Lancing giving her a puzzled look, and Jonas watching
her with a faint smile in his eyes.

"A penny for them," Melody said with a laugh.

"I was thinking about crime," Randi said, and the
butler dropped a glass on the floor.

XV

$\mathcal{A}$T ten-thirty, seeing the weariness in Jonas's face, Randi glanced at Melody, who nodded and got to her feet.

"Thank you for a delightful evening, Jonas," she said. "I think Randi and I must be getting home." She looked at Lancing. "What have you done about a babysitter, John?" She was unaware of the casual domestic tone, as though she and John Lancing had been making Andy their joint concern all his life.

"Luther managed to get me a girl from the village, because his wife is an early riser and doesn't like sitting up late. I promised to deliver her at her house before eleven."

While the girls were upstairs putting on their evening coats Melody said softly, "I understand so much better now. Jonas is a fine person. He deserves to be happy."

Randi smiled. "I knew you would understand once you met him."

For a moment Melody was tempted to mention the letter in her evening bag, but Jonas had given it to her with the implied pledge of secrecy.

When they went downstairs Jonas was standing in

the hallway with John and Cary, waiting to say good night to his guests. Luther, who had gone to open the front door, turned back and caught Cary's eye. Together the two men drifted casually toward the back of the hallway. The butler was saying something in a low, urgent voice.

"Sure about that?" Cary asked.

The butler nodded emphatically. "I always check on the doors, sir. I've never in all my years of service left one unlocked at night, let alone open. Just standing ajar it was, as though someone had been afraid of making a noise by shutting it."

"When did you notice this?"

"Just now when I was preparing for the young ladies to leave."

Quietly as the two men were talking, something in their attitude caught Jonas's attention.

"What's wrong, Cary?" he asked.

"Why — nothing, sir."

Jonas laughed. "Come on now. Something has happened. What is it?"

Cary hesitated, then shrugged and responded to Jonas's tone rather than his words. "Nothing, probably. Luther was disturbed because he just found the front door ajar. I think, if you have no objection, I'd like to go through the house and make a quick check."

"Looking for a burglar?" Jonas seemed amused rather than perturbed.

"Looking for something, at any rate," Cary said, without an answering smile. He collected Luther and John with a quick gesture. "We'll just look around. I wish you and the girls would stay in the drawing room, sir. That's one place that must be all right. No one could be lurking there because it has been occupied ever since dinner."

"Go ahead," Jonas said.

While Luther took the back of the house and John Lancing started with the small living room, Cary went up the stairs. They could hear him overhead in the library.

He was apparently searching the room foot by foot, not simply looking for an intruder. When Jonas became aware of the fact the smile faded from his face and his eyes narrowed in speculation.

"Send John up here," Cary called. "I have a hunch that whatever it is will be in Mr. King's own suite of rooms."

Randi found Lancing in the small living room and gave him Cary's message. It seemed to be only a moment before there was a shout, "Here it is, John!"

The two men were stamping around overhead. There was a queer acrid smell in the air. Luther raced up the stairs. Then from outside there came the sound of pounding feet and someone banged on the front door.

Randi ran to open it. Young Peters came in, dragging a breathless Sally with him.

"Fire!" he shouted. "I could see flames as we came up. Have you called the fire department?"

While Randi dialed the number, he ran up the stairs to join the other men. Jonas gasped for breath and sat down abruptly on a deep couch in the drawing room. Melody, whose air of fragility made her appear misleadingly helpless, took his wrist in her fingers and said crisply, "Sally, get a glass of water at once."

Jonas's lips moved in a husky whisper though almost no sound came out. Melody, watching him, nodded her comprehension. As Sally came running from the kitchen with a glass of water, Melody lifted Jonas's head gently and held the glass so he could swallow.

"Randi, in Mr. King's dressing room you will find a medicine bottle. See if you can get it for me right away."

Randi, who had returned from the telephone, saw Jonas's face parchment white, saw his attempt to smile at her. "The fire department is on its way," she said, and ran up the stairs.

As she opened the library door, Peters shouted a warning. "Keep that door shut. We don't want a draft through here."

Lancing, Cary, and Luther were beating out flames in the draperies and the carpet in Jonas's bedroom.

"There's a bottle of medicine in the dressing room," Randi said. "We must have it for Mr. King."

Peters hurried back, skirting the men who were working in frantic haste, found the bottle, and returned.

"Be sure to close that door behind you," he said.

She raced down the stairs and handed the bottle to Melody, who read the instructions, carefully measured out three drops into the glass of water.

"What's — going on up there?" Jonas said with difficulty.

"Someone set fire to the draperies in your bedroom. I

don't think there will be too much damage. There are four men to keep the fire under control. I think they caught it in time."

It seemed only a few minutes before there was the blood-chilling scream of the rise and fall of a siren. A fire engine stopped before the house. Behind it came the motley array of cars belonging to the members of the volunteer fire department: Cadillacs and Fords, Volkswagens and jeeps, even a couple of trucks.

Randi opened the door. "It's on the second floor at the back," she told the men, instructed Sally to stand at the door to admit and direct them, and went back to the drawing room to look anxiously at Jonas.

Melody smiled reassuringly at her. "He's better."

"But all this noise, this excitement —"

Jonas's lips moved and Randi leaned close to hear his words. "Hubert up to his old tricks?"

"I'm afraid so."

There was a jangle at the telephone and Randi went to answer it.

"Is this the Jonas King residence?"

"Yes."

"This is the state police. May I speak to Mr. King?"

"This is his fiancée, Randi Scott. There's a fire in the house, the men from the volunteer fire department are still arriving, and Mr. King is unable to answer the phone. The excitement has been too much for his heart."

There was an exclamation at the other end of the line. Then Lieutenant Barker said, "I'm on my way."

Randi telephoned Jonas's doctor and went back to close the door of the drawing room, attempting to shut out some of the turmoil: the sound of running feet, the crackling sound of flames, the pungent and choking billows of smoke.

She clasped Jonas's cold hand in her warm one and held it quietly. He managed to smile at her and at Melody, but he did not attempt to exhaust his strength by talking.

When she saw the blinking roof light of a squad car Randi went to admit the lieutenant. She saw him station a trooper to turn back the mob of curious bystanders who seem to emerge from cracks when anything happens. Lieutenant Barker's face was unexpectedly grim and hard when he did appear, and he went up the stairs at once, without talking to Randi. In a few moments the doctor arrived, and the two girls went into the smaller living room at the back of the house so he could examine his patient in privacy.

"I didn't know," Melody said at last, "it could be like this. I didn't dream it could be like this. I understand now why you have made up your mind to help Jonas to the best of your ability. Do you really believe his brother is responsible for the fire?"

"What terrifies me," Randi said slowly, "is that I may be responsible for it myself."

She heard a quickly indrawn breath and Cary walked into the room. His face was smudged with smoke, there were scorch marks on his dinner clothes. He was gray with fatigue.

"What —" she began eagerly.

"The fire seems to be out," he told her. "The men are checking to make sure there are no sparks and nothing smoldering, and then they will be ready to leave."

"The fire was deliberately set, wasn't it?"

"Oh, it was arson, all right. No doubt about that."

"What were you hunting for when you rushed up the stairs? A fire bomb?"

"I didn't really know. A booby trap of some sort. Luther found the front door ajar but I didn't believe there was a burglar in the place. I thought something had been done to startle or — or kill Mr. King. But whether it was a fire bomb or —" He lifted a tired hand, let it drop. Now his eyes were fixed on her face. "Why do you feel responsible?"

"Because I knew another attempt was going to be made to bring about a heart attack, a fatal attack."

"And it didn't occur to you to tell anyone?" His voice was hard and hostile.

Melody looked from one to the other. What had caused this naked enmity?

"I didn't have a chance. I just found out while I was dressing for dinner and I didn't want Jonas to know." Randi told him about Sally's attempt to steal the diamond bracelet because she wanted to get away. She had been planted in the house by Mavis Bertram and was terrified of Mavis.

"And what," asked a voice from the doorway, "did Miss Bertram expect to accomplish?"

Randi looked around in surprise.

"This is Lieutenant Barker," Cary said. "Miss Melody Scott and Miss Randi Scott."

The lieutenant looked from Randi to Melody, evidently unprepared for their beauty.

"And what's this about Miss Bertram?" he asked.

"Sally told me," Randi said. "Sally Murton. A new maid. She said she had been given the combination to Jonas's safe and that after he died of a heart attack she was to open the safe and steal his will. I — I didn't turn her over to you because she was so frightened. I thought she deserved another chance. But if I let this happen, if Sally was responsible for setting the fire, then I've made a terrible mistake. And yet I swear I don't believe she realized the implications or knew that Jonas's death was to be brought about deliberately."

Lieutenant Barker studied her thoughtfully, trying to sum up her quality. This was a girl who, after being proposed to by a wealthy man old enough to be her father, had broken a two-year engagement to another man. For some reason King had enormous faith in her integrity. But the story of Sally the maid struck him as unbelievable. He'd like to know a lot more about this beautiful girl before he could share King's faith in her.

"I'll talk to Sally later," he said. "It may be she was intended simply to rob the safe. I'm fairly sure that the fire was set here by the Bertram woman herself."

As Cary gave a sharp exclamation he said, "That is why I called tonight. The man I had following her lost track of her for a while and then saw her leaving this house less than an hour ago. She must have arranged to

have a key made while she was working here. Or else
Sally —"

"Sally didn't know anything about it, Lieutenant."

The lieutenant looked in surprise at the young man
who had just come in. "Who are you and what do you
know about this?"

Peters glanced at Randi. "Miss Scott can tell you
who I am."

"Anything she can do I can do better," John Lancing
laughed from the doorway. "I don't think we can keep
your identity a secret any longer, in the circumstances.
Lieutenant, this is Henry Peters. I told you about him,
remember? I said I was going to plant him here as a
kind of double-bluff to look after Mr. King."

"So you are the man." The lieutentant looked at him
for a moment. "Well, I suppose we can get this sorted
out sooner or later. What I can't figure is how the
Bertram woman got into this house and upstairs un-
seen. Unless the girl Sally or the butler —"

"Not Luther," Cary said firmly. "I put Luther in the
picture yesterday. He will do everything he can to
protect Mr. King."

"And not Sally," Peters said. "I took her to the
movies tonight and I got her life story. We didn't
return here until after the fire had started. And I doubt
if Sally held out a thing. She knew she was supposed to
rob the safe, but she didn't know about the arson."

"Your own position is rather unusual, isn't it?" the
lieutenant said mildly. "I've always lacked enthusiasm
for people who play both sides." If he saw the dull color

rise in young Peters's face, he ignored it. "I like men who take a clear stand."

"I explained all that to you," John Lancing said in defense of his friend. "Until he was wounded in Vietnam, Peters was working with Military Intelligence. He learned a lot about enemy methods of infiltration. When he came out of the hospital he looked me up because I had been carrying on a private war with the All-American Party and he wanted to help. This was, of course, before I had joined Cary's group, and at that time there didn't seem much that an individual could do. So I suggested that Peters take one of the enemy's tactics and use it himself. I wanted him to join the party and find out at first hand what they are doing, how they are operating, what they plan, so that we would be in a better position to block their moves."

"Suppose they find out?" the lieutenant asked.

"Then I'd be out of luck," Peters admitted cheerfully, "but as I understand it, about twenty percent of the members of the American Communist Party are actually FBI men who have infiltrated. It seems to work."

"Isn't it rather dangerous?"

"War is dangerous," Peters pointed out, "for the man in the field; increasingly so even for the civilian at home. War prevention is worth taking chances for."

"Oh!" Randi exclaimed to Peters. "That is why your face was so familiar. I saw you once before. You were with that young man who was attempting to organize the college students, trying to persuade them that the democratic method and respect for law do not work, that the only way to accomplish anything is by violence. Take over the country by force."

Peters grinned. "That was bad luck. I didn't expect the photographers to be there or I'd have been careful to keep in the background."

"Suppose you make your position clear. If you can." The lieutenant was still disapproving.

Peters looked at Lancing, his brows arched. Lancing nodded.

"Well, it's like this. As Mr. Lancing says, I saw how infiltration worked while I was in Vietnam. It's insidious. It's almost impossible to detect. It's dangerous but it is terribly effective. So I got in touch with Lancing after I read an article he had written about this party that is so hell-bent on stirring up young people, getting them to organize, getting them to shout slogans and generally give the impression abroad that we are a nation that cannot rule its own people, and of a people unfit for democracy and self-government. All this annoys me."

Something in the absurd understatement made the lieutenant laugh and some of his suspicion faded.

"Well, we didn't know at the time how far Mr. Hamilton had gone — he's way ahead of us, of course — so we were working more or less on our own. Then, at Mr. Lancing's suggestion, I got into the party."

"How?" the lieutenant wanted to know.

Peters grinned. "Oh, that was easy. I waited until I heard someone say the country is on the skids, that our police and our judges and our courts and our whole system of government by law was corrupt, that you can accomplish more by Molotov cocktails and sniping from roofs at innocent bystanders than by the intelligent use of the vote and open discussion. What they were selling was government by terror. Then I piped up and said, 'Me too,' and they welcomed me like a brother. They thought I was a Big Brain like them.

"Well, I came here because of the student riots. I wondered who was back of them. It was easy to discover that Mr. Hubert King is running the show in this vicinity. So I scraped up an acquaintance with him, convinced him I was a fellow traveler, and he put me to work. It was on that college campus that Miss Scott must have seen the picture of me. I'm not supposed to be identified with them, of course. The way they operate is that each one of us is supposed to be an indignant citizen working on his own for the welfare of his country.

"Then Mr. Lancing told me about the curious setup of the Kings, brother against brother. He wanted someone in this house to protect Mr. King. The idea sort of amused me. So I told Hubert that I'd like a more active role. It was a pity that my only skills were typing and shorthand. Well, that did it. He had the brilliant idea of getting me in here to replace Miss Scott, which, of course, was exactly what I was aiming at."

"Have you encountered any other members of Hubert's group or cell or whatever they call them?"

"As I explained, we don't fraternize much. There is

the guy I worked with on that college deal — and what dopes those kids were to fall for the kind of baloney they were told! His name is Manton. He comes from some orphanage and Hubert gave him his job when he was eighteen. Is he indoctrinated!" Peters shook his head. "Whatever Hubert tells him he believes. Hubert is the great man."

"Have you met a lawyer named Willis Jameson in Mr. Hubert King's organization?" Randi asked.

Cary turned sharply as he heard the question, staring at her. He looked, Melody thought, as though he hated her sister.

"Jameson? What's he like?"

"About twenty-seven, fair, very good-looking," Randi said.

Peters shook his head. "I don't know anyone who fits that description myself, but that's no proof one way or another. Well, there's that woman, Mavis Bertram, the nurse whom Hubert planted here. Then, of course, they got hold of poor little Sally."

"What's your opinion of Sally?" the lieutenant asked.

"I turned her inside out tonight, sir. She is really a trusting soul!" Peters shook his head. "She shouldn't be allowed out."

A quavering voice said, "Mr. King asked me to tell you that the doctor has just left." Sally gave a long, bitter, disillusioned look at Peters and went out of the room.

Men were trooping down the stairs. Jonas, standing at the door of the drawing room, insisted on shaking hands with each of them and thanking them personally. Luther came in, pulling on his jacket. Except for smudges on his cheek he looked as correct as usual.

"I don't believe you can use your bedroom until it is thoroughly aired and freed of smoke, sir. Shall I have the bed in the front guest suite prepared for you? My wife and the housekeeper are both waiting to do anything that you want."

"Whatever you like," Jonas said wearily.

Randi turned to Cary, a challenge in her voice. "What could I have done?" she demanded.

"About Jameson?" He looked and sounded like a stranger.

"About Willis?" She was taken aback, puzzled. "No, of course not. About Sally."

"Surely that is up to you," he said. He turned to John. "I suggest we let Luther get some rest as he has to be on the job tomorrow. We'll take turns guarding the place tonight."

"Good," Lancing said. "That suits me fine."

"How about me?" Peters asked eagerly.

"You weren't supposed to show up until tomorrow. You had better stick to your schedule."

"Well, that may be just as well, as brother Hubert will expect some kind of report on the fire."

"Tell him," Cary said, "that Mr. King has collapsed as a result of the excitement and that he is in serious condition."

"Would you mind taking my baby-sitter home?" Lancing asked Peters.

"If you are both going to be on guard in the house all night, perhaps I had better ask her to stay with the little boy. I can explain to her family."

"Fine."

"Then suppose," Cary suggested, "you drive Miss Scott and her sister home."

He turned away without another look at Randi.

XVI

THE movie was a musical comedy with lilting music, beautiful clothes, and a gay story. Sally found herself laughing, turning to exchange delighted glances with Hal Peters, sharing her pleasure with him.

For two hours she completely forgot the problems that had seemed insurmountable that afternoon, the despair that had driven her, the stupid frantic attempt to steal the bracelet, Miss Scott's unexpected kindness. She lived in the glittering fairytale of the musical comedy, she wore the glamorous dresses, she was the object of the handsome hero's adoration, she joined wholeheartedly in the audience's shouts of laughter.

As a rule, the ending of a movie left her feeling rather flat, jerked out of her dream world, aware of the vast difference between the glamorous movie star and her own drab self. But tonight the illusion of gaiety and happiness did not end with the movie.

"Let's get something to eat," Hal Peters suggested. He helped her into a shabby old car with as much gallantry as though it were a Rolls, and she settled back in delight. At a roadside stand they ordered ham-

burgers and coffee, and Sally, who had been too upset
to touch her dinner, ate with a healthy appetite.

Across the table Hal smiled at her. He talked easily
about the movie they had just seen and described an
entertainment that had been given to the boys in Vietnam, played against a background of machine guns and
rifle fire. He had never found a girl so easy to entertain,
and he was both amused and touched by the flattering
attention she gave to each word.

Before long he was telling her a funny story about
his childhood and, without quite knowing how, she
found herself telling him about hers, about the father
who had sometimes been kind and sometimes cruel,
about the loneliness of a house with no woman in it and
no companions of her own age; of her father's arrest
and imprisonment and the bleak years in the orphanage.

She had never talked so much about herself in her
whole life and it gave her a curious sense of deliverance.
At the same time she felt that this quiet young man
with the observant eyes understood and sympathized.

Back in the car, he drove in a leisurely way as though
he too were in no hurry to bring this evening to an end.
His manner was still casual and friendly. Before he
reached the King house he stopped the car and reached
for her hand. He did not try to kiss her. He simply held
her hand, warm and safe, in his own.

"It hasn't been much fun for you, has it, little Sally?"
he said gently.

The unexpected kindness brought tears to her eyes.
"No, but it's going to be better now," she said. "Miss

Scott is so nice. And she won't let Them hurt me. She promised."

"Them?"

Sally responded to his interest like a bud to water. She blossomed. She told him about Mavis offering her a job when she left the orphanage and then changing, becoming a frightening woman. She had said Sally must take the job at Jonas King's. She had provided fake references. She had said that Sally was to steal Mr. King's will after he died of a heart attack and had given her the combination of the safe in the library. So Sally had been afraid. She wanted to run away, to escape from the woman who threatened her with prison if she did not obey her orders.

"So tonight I tried to steal Miss Scott's diamond bracelet while she was taking a bath." Sally told him what had happened. "I didn't know people could be so good. I just wouldn't of believed it."

"But now you do." He pressed her hand, smiling at her.

She smiled back. "Now I do!"

He had been looking past her, toward the great bulk of the King house. Suddenly he gave a sharp exclamation. "Fire! My God, the house is on fire!"

He put the car in gear, roared up the driveway and shut off the motor. He got out, dragging Sally with him as he ran to the house.

Now Sally could see the flames in an upstairs window, see shadowy figures beating at them. When she got in the house she found Mr. King in a state of collapse and a beautiful girl who must be Miss Scott's sister bending over him in concern. At her request Sally ran for water and then Miss Randi asked her to stand at the outside door to admit the members of the volunteer fire department, who hastened up the stairs, working with disciplined speed. Sally heard the crackling of flames, smelled choking smoke.

Then a lieutenant from the state police was there. He said that Miss Bertram had been seen leaving the house. Sally knew then that it was she who had set the fire. For the first time she understood why Miss Bertram had been so sure that Mr. King would have a heart attack.

Then she heard the lieutenant ask Hal, "What's your opinion of Sally?" And Hal had replied, "I turned her inside out tonight, sir. She's really a trusting soul! She shouldn't be allowed out."

I'll never trust anyone again, Sally thought bitterly. Never again. I should of known someone like that wasn't interested in me. He was just trying to find out about me for the police. And he seemed so nice. I liked him so much. So very much.

She cried herself to sleep.

ii

"Suppose," Cary suggested, "I take the first watch. I'll wake you about three." He smiled at Lancing. "After all, you have to be up in the morning to deliver Andy to Melody, and I can do my sleeping then."

"Fine." Lancing agreed.

The housekeeper had hastily made up a bed in the front guest suite for Jonas, and his valet reported that he was already sleeping quietly. In the sitting room of the suite, Lancing removed shoes, loosened his necktie, and stretched out on a comfortable down sofa. He too was asleep within ten minutes.

Cary eased the door open and paced up and down the wide hall. It had taken the fire to make him realize the extent of Hubert's ruthless determination to destroy his brother and get his hands on the King fortune. Thank God, he thought fervently, Jonas had come through the shock of the ordeal as well as he had.

Tonight Hubert would be told by Peters that his brother's condition was serious. Perhaps he would make no further attempt to injure him. In any case, with Peters and Luther on constant alert in the house, nothing could happen. Two more days. Surely they could keep Jonas safe for two more days.

He wondered how much of Sally's story was true. Was she really as innocent of the attempt to start a fire as she had appeared to be? Jonas must change the combination of his safe in the morning, and the lock on the front door. The Bertram woman seemed to be able to enter the house at will.

"But what should I have done?" Randi had cried. And he had replied bitterly, "About Jameson?"

Very good-looking was the way she had described her former fiancé. She had been engaged to him for two years and had broken that engagement as soon as Jonas proposed to her.

I can't be that wrong about her, Cary thought, as he strode up and down, up and down, the long hallway. He remembered her clear honest eyes. She can't be dishonest. But how could he account for that broken engagement? Jealousy, Cary had always thought, was a contemptible trait, but at the moment he was consumed by jealousy and he knew it, yet was helpless to prevent it. He would have liked to smash the face of the "very good-looking" Willis Jameson. He wondered if Randi knew that Willis had a reputation for playing the field. How he would like to tell her!

"This is love with honor," he had told her and he had meant it. But that was before he knew of the existence of the very good-looking Willis Jameson. And Randi had been with the man in that dark garden. John Lancing hadn't wanted to tell him about Randi's ex-fiancé, but of course he had had to. What kind of game were the two of them playing?

The worst of it was, Cary admitted to himself, that whether or not she was honest, whether or not she was interested in King's money, whether or not she was still infatuated with Jameson, he loved her. For keeps.

In the thirty years of his life Cary had learned to feel that he was the master of his fate, that he could handle events as he saw fit. Now he was helpless. Well, he would stay on at the guesthouse until the wedding was over and Jonas was safe, and then he would clear out. He would go to the ends of the earth if it was necessary. But he would avoid Randi Scott as he would the plague. It was all that he could do for his own peace of mind.

The only trouble with that was that nothing seemed worthwhile without her. There was nothing to look forward to.

Sunk in his bitter thoughts, he was startled by Lancing's hand on his arm. "Hey, you were going to call me at three. It's after six. You've been on guard all night."

Cary looked at him blankly for a moment. "I forgot," he said. "Anyhow, I can sleep all day."

iii

Peters opened the car door for Randi and Melody. Neither of the girls had spoken since they had left Jonas King's house. He looked anxiously from one white face to the other.

"Are you sure you girls are going to be all right?"

"Oh, yes," Randi assured him. "We are tired, of course, and shocked. But we'll be all right."

"Did the baby-sitter mind staying on for the night?" Melody inquired.

"No, I think she was thrilled by all the excitement. She's just a kid but she seems reliable. The housekeeper took her out some night things, and she is really enjoying herself."

He waited until the two girls had gone inside the cottage and had flashed on and off the porch light to assure him that all was well. Then he drove on to Hubert King's house, which was several miles beyond the village and at the top of a hill. The approach was difficult in winter because of the steep road, but there

was a beautiful view from the summit. Sometimes
Peters suspected that Hubert enjoyed a feeling that he
could, literally, look down on his fellowmen.

Unlike the old family home, Hubert's house was
starkly modern. He had paid a great deal more than he
could afford for it, but he needed the outward signs of
affluence for reassurance.

Tonight the house was a blaze of lights, and Peters
realized that his heartbeat had accelerated. This would
be the first time that he had attended a gathering of the
members of the action committee, the first time he
would see other members of the group.

The door was opened by a hard-faced man who was
both houseman and bodyguard, though no one had ever
threatened Hubert. The party lived in such a state of
conspiracy that its members believed other people were
as hostile and belligerent as they were.

The room seemed to be filled with people, though
there were only half a dozen.

Hubert came to shake hands with Peters.

"I hope you don't mind my coming without an
appointment," Peters said, as the rule was that members should not encounter each other except under
unusual circumstances.

"No, glad to have you." Hubert grinned. Obviously
he was in high spirits. "We've been having a box seat
for the stage show." He nodded his head toward the
window. Peters joined him there and realized that from
this height there had been a clear view over the village
to Jonas's house.

"Quite a fire," Hubert said in a tone of satisfaction. "Did you see it?"

As it was against the rules for Peters to go out with Sally and he was not even supposed to know that the two of them were taking orders from the same group, he did not refer to her. "That's why I came to report," he said. "I saw the fire and mingled with the volunteer firemen to find out what was going on."

"Good work," Hubert said. "How much damage?"

"Not too much damage; nothing, that is, that can't be repaired or replaced. But Mr. King suffered a heart attack. The doctor was still there when I left. I understand that the situation is serious, perhaps even critical."

Hubert made a grimace of mock sorrow. "Too, too bad," he said mournfully, and there was a general laugh. "I guess," and he made no attempt to conceal his satisfaction, "that will take care of our bridegroom."

Peters looked around curiously, saw a tall blond woman who was almost beautiful, a woman who wore a stunning emerald ring.

"This is Miss Bertram," Hubert said. "Mr. Peters, who has just joined our party and is a very promising recruit. Miss Bertram is tonight's heroine. She had a key made to Jonas's house and got in there this evening to set the fire. A very nice device timed so that dear Jonas would be asleep."

Mavis Bertram's eyes rested on Peter's face in a flattering way. "Mr. Peters," she cooed, "it will be a pleasure working with you."

"And Willis Jameson," Hubert said.

Willis tossed back a long lock of hair that had fallen over his forehead and shook hands with Peters. So this was the very good-looking man whom Randi Scott had mentioned as probably belonging to the All-American Party. Peters, summing him up rapidly, wondered what on earth that fine girl had seen in the man. Good-looking? Yes. But there was no character, no decision, no imagination or intelligence or kindness in his face. It was the face of a self-indulgent and conceited puppy.

"Manton you know, of course, because you've worked together before," Hubert said.

The boy was slight, with a straggly beard and fanatical eyes behind dark glasses. The two nodded to each other.

There were two other young men, not over twenty, and Peters began to suspect that, like Sally and Manton, they had been recruited when they left an orphanage, carefully indoctrinated, and put to work by Hubert.

"I suppose," Hubert said, "there was a great deal of confusion during the fire."

"Not really," Peters told him. "Of course there was a lot of activity in Mr. King's suite of rooms, but the firemen seemed to know their job."

Hubert nodded thoughtfully. "I don't often like having any association, any public link, between the members of the action committee. In fact, up to now, as you know, I have preferred not to have them meet. But in this case I think you should know we have someone else planted in Jonas's house."

Peters looked at him in bland surprise. "Indeed, sir!"

"Lady's maid, girl named Sally Murton. Mavis had it fixed up and she has briefed the girl. Sally has a job to do for us as soon as — that is, if anything should happen to Jonas. If she needs your help, I expect you to provide it."

"Anything!" Peters said in the fervent tone of a convert. "Anything at all!"

"Good." Hubert said. "Well, if there is nothing else — you can go now. All of you except —" Hubert looked around. "Manton, I'll want you."

The fanatical face lighted up. "Yes, sir," Manton said eagerly.

Peters felt a pang of pity. The boy was so young, so untaught. It never occurred to him that he was merely a tool. There must be some way to save him before his own actions made it too late, before he had strayed too far beyond the law. It occurred to Peters, with wry humor, that probably Cary Hamilton, whom the boy regarded as an enemy, would be the one most likely to help him.

"There isn't room in this world for both Cary Hamilton and me," Hubert said. He waved a peremptory hand, dismissing the others. As they trooped obediently to the door, Peters heard Hubert say, "Now then, Manton —"

The door was closed behind them by the grim-faced servant who doubled as bodyguard.

A car started up. Mavis Bertram began to run. "Willis," she called urgently, ran in front of the Volkswagen, forcing Jameson to stop, climbed in beside him.

With a hasty good night, Peters got into his own car and drove off. Not far from the house he passed the Volkswagen drawn up at the side of the road. Inside, he could see Mavis gesticulating eagerly and Willis staring ahead bleakly.

For ten or fifteen minutes Peters drove with apparent absentmindedness along country roads where he could see whether or not he was followed. When he was sure there was no one watching him he drove rapidly to the state police barracks.

Lieutenant Barker was working on a report. "What — oh, you are Peters, aren't you?"

"Yes. I'd like to talk to you, if I may."

"Can it wait? I have a report to get out."

"I'm not sure that it can wait," Peters admitted, "and I may not be free later to come to you in person without being seen."

"Afraid?" The lieutenant's tone was caustic.

"Once I'm unmasked I won't be of much use, will I?" Peters said mildly.

The lieutenant put down his pen and lighted a cigarette. "Go ahead." He motioned to a policeman to take notes.

Peters described the meeting of the All-American Party's action committee at Hubert King's; described the people whom he had seen there.

"Hubert means business," Peters concluded. "He is not only responsible for Mavis Bertram setting fire to his brother's house but he intends to eliminate Hamilton and Lancing if he can, because he knows they will fight him to the bitter end."

"What do you think he has in mind?"

"Violence," Peters said succinctly. "This is not merely a case for shock treatment as it was with his brother. This is a case of silencing two men permanently. I don't honestly believe I could overstate the danger which they are in at this moment."

"We'll set up a guard in the guesthouse itself," Barker decided. "Anything else?"

"Well, I'm not sure about this, but I think one way Hubert is recruiting is by taking youngsters when they leave an orphanage at eighteen, indoctrinating them, and putting them to work. That's what happened to young Manton. With poor little Sally they are trying to use blackmail and terror. There were two other kids there tonight, all fervent and dedicated."

"How," the lieutenant exploded wrathfully, *"how* did this happen here? A quiet, peaceful, law-abiding community, with no real poverty, nothing to spark even the most neurotic into violence."

"I guess maybe," Peters said, "not enough people care about what happens to their community. They think it doesn't concern them. Or perhaps it isn't the people who are at fault. After all, the ones who make trouble are only a handful. But the guns make more noise than the peaceful people, the shouters make more noise than the quiet-spoken. Look at the assassinations in this country in the last few years. Committed by fanatics and psychotics. But though the rest of the world may think that violence is typical of us we know it's true only of a few. We must not think they are all like that. Most people are men of goodwill."

"We have a job cut out for us, clearing this thing up."

"At least," Peters said, "it is worth doing."

XVII

"WELL, I didn't expect to see you up!" Mrs. Echo exclaimed. "I thought you'd be sleeping half the day."

"Why?" Randi asked in surprise. Half the day? She had barely closed her eyes all night long. This morning they were shadowed and her mouth twitched with nerves.

"That fire at Mr. King's. It's all over town. Arson, I hear. And Mr. King is in dreadful shape and not expected to live on account of shock and a heart attack and all. Poor man. How did it happen?"

She was a kindly woman and her avid curiosity was, after all, only natural, Randi told herself. She laughed. "I'm surprised you haven't heard that too."

"Well, there's stories," Mrs. Echo said darkly, "and the truth will get around, sooner or later. Things always do in this town. Like my husband says, truth will out. I don't know when we've had such goings-on. Do you know the state police have been going over the scaffolding on the new building on Main Street and found out that the rope was cut? Deliberately cut! Someone out to sabotage the work. Maybe Communists."

Randi laughed. "Why on earth would Communists want to cause an accident to a small building in a small village?"

"You'll see for yourself," Mrs. Echo warned her. "There's a young man parading outside the building now with a placard saying, 'Don't let the Communists destroy our town.' "

"Was he wearing a sheet and a hood?"

"You needn't laugh. Thank goodness, we've got some people in this town who know what's what. I hear you and Miss Melody had dinner at Mr. King's. All dressed up fit to kill."

"How in the world," Randi asked in amusement, "did you hear that?"

"Well, my goodness, my husband belongs to the volunteer fire department, and he knows you both by sight. Two prettiest girls in town, he always says."

"Don't bother with a tray for Melody this morning. I'll call her in a few minutes and we'll both have breakfast downstairs. We're going out later."

"She looks a heap better every day, doesn't she? Lately I think she tries to do half my work and now she is looking after that little boy. A regular picture, he is, but a handful. The way Miss Melody is blossoming out anyone would think she was in love, only I can't figure out who it would be. I always used to think she'd marry before you did — not just because she is older, but she's a born homemaker, that one."

The older woman's eye fell on the diamond solitaire blazing on Randi's slender hand. "Well, so he got around to it at last, did he?" she said in a tone that brought color rushing into Randi's face. It was apparent that Mrs. Echo, like Melody, had not trusted Willis Jameson's devotion to her, had not believed he wanted to marry her. Randi turned away and ran up to tap on Melody's door.

"Come in," Melody called. "I've been up for half an hour and I've already bathed and dressed. I've been planning just what I want to do about the altar in the drawing room for your wedding. Perhaps we had better stop at a florist's on the way to the house. I called John and told him not to bring Andy this morning because I'll be there decorating for you. Do you think Jonas would mind if I keep Andy with me in the drawing room?"

"Not if you can keep him in order. If you can manage to prevent him from howling and getting in a tantrum it would be fine, but Jonas should not be exposed to much more noise and excitement."

"Andy won't howl," Melody said firmly.

Randi looked at her, shook her head, and laughed. "No one seeing you would believe you have this hard core of discipline. You look about as firm as a hummingbird."

Soon after breakfast a car door slammed and John Lancing came up on the porch. He helped the girls into Jonas's Buick, and at Melody's request drove to a florist's. As they passed the building under construction Randi saw the boy with the placard. He was very young, not more than twenty, with heavy dark glasses and a rather thin beard that made him look much younger than his actual age.

"So that's the way Hubert is playing it!" John said grimly. "Found a scapegoat. Well, it worked with Mussolini and Hitler. Why not here?"

When they reached the King house, Luther came out, followed by Peters, and they carried in the daffodils and yellow tulips. Plants and greens were to be delivered later by truck. Jonas King and Cary Hamilton, Peters told them, were still sleeping, Jonas in the front guest suite, and Cary in the guesthouse.

"Did you really believe anything more would happen during the night?" Randi asked.

"It's always better not to take a chance," John said. "There is just one more day. Tomorrow is your wedding, and after that everything should be all right."

The housekeeper had left word with Luther that she would like to discuss the damage in Mr. King's rooms with Miss Scott as soon as possible so that repairs could be made without delay. Leaving Melody with a delighted John at work in the drawing room, while Andy looked on entranced by the activity, Randi followed the housekeeper through the library and into Jonas's dressing room and bedroom.

The damage had been limited chiefly to the bedroom, where the draperies at the window, the bedding, the carpet, had been burned. The walls were scorched. The room was filled with the acrid odor of smoke although the windows had been opened wide.

"The insurance man has already been here to assess

the damage," Mrs. Wilkes said. "Apparently some sort of timing device was used. The fire was intended to catch the draperies here, you see. Evidently it was assumed that Mr. King would be in bed, as he usually is, by ten, and that he would be asleep when the fire started. A truly diabolical thing! If shock had not brought on a heart attack he would probably have been overcome by smoke. Thank God, he was entertaining and there were able-bodied men in the house who were prepared to help."

Randi found herself shaking. "I didn't know people could be so evil. And Jonas is so good. We'll protect him from now on if we have to stand guard every single minute."

The housekeeper smiled at the girl's challenging tone, at the carriage of her head. "If anyone can look after him, Miss Scott, I think you are the one to do it. I'm so glad for him." She added frankly, "You know, at first I didn't think it could possibly be a good marriage but I was mistaken. I'm so glad I was!"

"We'll make it a good marriage," Randi said, and it was a promise. "Now first," and her voice was brisk, almost gay, "we'll have the draperies — what's left of them — taken down, the carpet removed, and get in painters and someone to refinish the floor. We'll have to order new carpeting from New York or Boston. There won't be anything suitable here in the village."

At the desk in the library she made out lists and telephoned orders with a crisp competence that surprised the housekeeper.

Meanwhile, down in the drawing room Melody was directing John Lancing and Peters and a man who usually worked in the garden, in setting up an altar near the fireplace and banking it with flowers. Andy, beside himself with excitement, kept getting involved with plants, with stepladders, with flowers.

Peters and the gardener went out to bring in the masses of greenery that had just arrived from the florist.

"So you see," Melody explained to John, "even if it should be gray and rainy tomorrow, this room will seem to be bright and sunlit because of the yellow tulips and the daffodils. A wedding should be sunny."

"What's a wedding?" Andy demanded.

"A wedding," Melody explained, "is when a man and a woman take a vow that they will love and honor each other forever and ever, and live as man and wife."

"I want to go to a wedding," Andy announced.

"You can go to a wedding tomorrow if you'll be very good and not make a single sound," Melody told him.

"Can I make a lot of sounds now to make up for it?" asked Andy, always the opportunist.

"I told you before that Mr. King must rest. If you are to play in this house you must be quiet so he can sleep."

"I won't be quiet!"

Melody did not argue the matter. "That's too bad," she said sadly. "I like having you here when you are good. John, will you please ring? . . . Oh, Luther, will you be good enough to take Andy out to the

kitchen. Your wife said she would keep an eye on him if
he didn't know how to behave in here."

When the little boy had been led away, dragging his
feet reluctantly, John said, "Melody, what am I going
to do about the boy? He's so spoiled, so undisciplined."

Melody laughed up at him. "Don't worry so much,
John. Nothing has been done to him that can't be un-
done with a little time and patience."

"Your time? Your patience?"

When she looked at him in surprise, he came to kneel
beside her. "Melody, Andy needs you. He is going to
need you for a long time. I don't want to have you leave
him."

She was very still. Some of the gaiety had died out of
her lovely face. The corners of her mouth drooped as
though in disappointment.

"Am I asking too terribly much?"

She bent over, her face concealed, carefully setting a
vase of daffodils in front of a mass of dark-green
foliage. "You want me to go on looking after Andy?"
she asked, her voice muffled.

He studied her half-hidden face anxiously. Then his
eyes widened, he began to laugh softly. "It isn't just
Andy," he told her. "I thought I was putting forward
my best sales talk, that you would be more likely to
respond to my small son's needs than to mine. But I'm
the one who wants you most, who needs you most,
Melody. For always. It isn't just a companion for my
son I am seeking, it is a beloved wife."

The great dark-fringed eyes were raised to his now.

"But John, you don't really know me at all; only a few meetings, only a few hours."

"I took one look at you," he said. "Just one look. And I fell in love with you. Cary knows it. I think Randi guesses it. I wish the whole world could be told about it. I'd like to shout it aloud. I'm so awfully in love with you, Melody. Could you learn to love me?"

Somehow she was in his arms. "I took just one look too," she said softly.

It was a long time before the work on the altar was resumed.

ii

Jonas's valet nodded to Peters, who had been waiting in the sitting room of the front guest suite.

"Mr. King will be glad to see you now."

Jonas, bathed and shaved and wearing a thin dark-blue silk dressing gown, was stretched out on a chaise longue. He looked surprisingly well in spite of the shock and strain of the night before.

"Good morning," he said pleasantly. "I haven't any instructions for you today as I want to conserve my strength. You might as well get settled in. Mrs. Wilkes tells me she has prepared two rooms for you on the third floor, a bedroom and an adjoining room you can use as a study or private sitting room. Whatever you like. The arrangements had to be made rather hurriedly, what with all the changes going on here and the complications caused by the fire, but if you don't find your quarters satisfactory now, you can suggest any alterations you would like when we have all settled down a bit."

"Thank you very much, sir. I'm glad to see you looking so well after last night's ordeal. But I didn't come for instructions this morning. I came to give you some information. But first I have two rather urgent suggestions: one is that you have the lock on the front door changed today; the other is that you have the combination of your safe changed at once. It seems that while she was working here, Miss Bertram had a key made for the front door and somehow she got hold of the combination to your safe."

"A very efficient young woman." Jonas was watching his new secretary keenly. "And may I ask how you got hold of this extraordinary information?"

Peters had an engaging grin. "Well, the lid was blown off last night, sir, so you might as well know the truth. I'm a colleague of John Lancing's. He got me to come to the village to infiltrate the — uh — your brother's organization." He looked rather uncomfortably at his employer.

"I know about my brother's activities," Jonas assured him dryly.

"Well, when Mr. Lancing learned that you were in danger, he suggested trying a double-bluff, and dropping enough hints so that your brother Hubert would suggest getting me into the house here. Then I'd be in a position to look after you but Hubert would think it was his own idea. That is why I was so anxious to move in at once, so I could be on the spot in case anything happened."

Jonas smiled broadly. "You know, when you first showed up I figured out there was something wrong with this picture. You simply didn't look like the kind of person to belong in Hubert's camp." He held out his hand. "I must say," he admitted frankly, "I'll be glad to have you around. It looks as though I am going to need someone." He frowned. "But after last night's fire I wonder whether I am justified in marrying Randi and bringing her into this house."

"Miss Scott will be safe, sir," Peters assured him.

"What's your own opinion about the fire?"

"As I said, Miss Bertram had a key made for the front door. She slipped in and set a timing device to start burning the curtains in your bedroom after you were asleep."

"So that's it!"

"And now if you'll give orders for a new door key and a new combination for your safe —"

"I don't keep money in there," Jonas said. "Nothing but a few papers — oh, of course, my will! You'll have to say for Hubert that he never gives up."

"Somehow," Peters said, "I doubt if you will be his target again. I reported to him last night that you had collapsed as a result of shock and that your condition was critical."

Jonas looked amused. "You seem to have had a busy evening." Then the look of amusement faded. "You said you doubted that I would be Hubert's target again. Just what did you have in mind, Peters?"

Peters cursed himself for his carelessness. "Nothing in particular, sir," he lied blandly.

iii

Peters started into the drawing room and halted abruptly when he saw John Lancing holding Melody Scott in his arms, saw her arms creep around his shoulders.

"Oh, darling, darling," John was whispering.

"John, my love."

Peters withdrew, smiling to himself, and shook his head at the gardener who was coming through the hall, his arms filled with plants.

"Not now," he said softly. "You and I aren't needed in there."

In the library on the second floor he made telephone calls to insure that the front-door lock would be changed and found a man from the safe-manufacturing company who promised to call in the late afternoon.

Peters let himself out and went around the house toward the little Swiss chalet. Yesterday he had encountered Sally here after that ugly interview she had had with Mavis Bertram. He remembered with a pang the bitter disillusionment in the girl's face when she had overheard his comments about her to Lieutenant Barker. He had hurt her terribly and she had already been hurt enough. Such a pathetic little waif, as easily amused as a child, and so grateful for small kindnesses. Surely he had not said anything that she could not forgive if he could make her understand. He owed her that.

As he passed the clump of bushes behind which he

had concealed himself while Sally and Mavis were talking, a hand gripped his arm, swung him around. He found himself facing a nondescript young man, with a hand like iron and a grim face.

"Who are you," the stranger demanded, "and where are you going?"

"Any reason why I should answer your questions?"

The man flipped open his wallet.

"State police!" Peters exclaimed. "Lieutenant Barker didn't waste any time. I'm Peters."

"Oh, yes, I've heard about you. Anything new?"

Peters shook his head. "We're having the lock on the front door changed today and the combination to the safe in the library. Take it all in all, Mr. King looks fine. Everything seems to be under control."

"What do you think is in the cards?" The trooper looked at the compact young man with the military carriage, the direct eyes, and liked what he saw. A good man to have on his side of the fence.

"I don't know," Peters admitted. "But I doubt if there will be any more attacks on Mr. King. His brother believes he is in terrible condition, so it would hardly be worthwhile to make another attempt and it would only arouse suspicion. So far, I doubt if Hubert knows anyone even guesses what he is up to. I think his next target will be Hamilton or Lancing. Hamilton is the most powerful and outspoken enemy the All-American Party has."

"My name is Grant," the trooper told him. "Where are these two guys I'm supposed to be guarding?"

Peters grinned. "Lancing is in the main house, in the drawing room, and from the look of things when I went past the door just now he is fully occupied. In fact, I think he is getting himself engaged to be married."

Grant scowled. "I don't much like that," he said.

Peters laughed aloud. "Why on earth not?"

"A man in love isn't reasonable," Grant complained. "He has his head in the clouds and he is not likely to look after himself. Where's the other one?"

"Hamilton? He is in the guesthouse and probably he is still asleep."

"Who is still asleep?" Cary had come across the lawn so quietly that neither man had been aware of his approach. "What's going on here?"

Peters introduced the two men and explained the situation briefly. "It's my belief that Hubert is going to change his tactics and let brother Jonas alone. You are his target now."

Cary, who had been strolling between the two men toward the little Swiss chalet, stopped abruptly. His face was dead white. "I see," he said at last. He made an effort at control. "Well, what do you have in mind?"

"My idea," Grant said, "is that until we can figure out what Hubert is up to, Peters will spend the days in the guesthouse, in case anyone tries to plant another booby trap, but keep out of sight, of course. I'll take over at night. I understand there is plenty of room in the big house so that Mr. Hamilton and Mr. Lancing can sleep there. But for heaven's sake, Peters, move carefully and keep away from the windows. I don't want Hubert to know you are in the guesthouse. The same thing goes for you, Mr. Hamilton. When you come across to the big house at night don't make a sound. The maid Sally is working for your brother and she'll report on your presence here if she finds out about you."

"No she won't," Peters said. "I'll take care of that."

"I don't like the way this thing is shaping up," Cary said. "I don't like the idea of you being a stand-in for me and taking the rap — if any."

"It's what I'm paid for," Grant told him. "It's my job. I'll be in no danger. In any case, to be quite frank about it, you are an important figure here. It would be very helpful if you were to cooperate with the police about this instead of opposing us."

"All right." Cary held out his hand. "And thank you."

Grant nodded. "I'll be around," he promised, "but you won't see me. I hope."

XVIII

SUNLIGHT poured through the windows of the drawing room and touched the altar with its massed daffodils and yellow tulips, which were like bottled sunshine. In the small living room beyond, a string quartet played softly. Before the altar stood a clergyman in his robes, and near him Jonas King waited with a white-faced Cary at his side.

In the guest suite at the back of the house Sally was fastening a zipper on Randi's wedding dress, her small face intent and eager. Melody, exquisite in the long turquoise silk sheath bridesmaid's dress that matched her lovely eyes, carefully adjusted the cap veil over Randi's dark hair. She stood back, smiling, though her eyes were misty.

"You're a beautiful bride, Randi."

Randi made herself return Melody's smile. "You will be too," she said. "Oh, Melody, I'm so happy about it! When do you plan to marry John?"

"Right away. He doesn't like the idea of my living alone in the cottage."

"But you could come here. There are plenty of rooms

on the third floor until Jonas can move back to his own suite and then —" She broke off as Melody shook her head.

"Actually —" Melody began.

Randi laughed. "It's John who doesn't want to live alone. I understand. Well, you can leave Andy here with me when you go on your honeymoon."

There was a tap at the sitting room door and Sally went to open it. John Lancing was waiting with Jonas's lawyer. As Melody came into the sitting room, Billings looked at her, his eyes widening as he studied that lovely face.

"Is this the bride?"

"This," John said, "is going to be my bride. Melody Scott. Darling, will you tell Randi —" Down below, the music swelled triumphantly into the wedding march.

Randi appeared in the doorway, slender and beautiful in the unadorned white wedding dress.

"This" John told her smiling, "is Mr. Billings, who is to give away the bride."

The lawyer looked at the steady eyes, saw the proud carriage of the head, the character and tenderness of the soft mouth.

"How very kind of you, Mr. Billings," Randi said as she held out her hand.

"It is my privilege, Miss Scott." Unexpectedly the shrewd face warmed. "I congratulate Jonas King with all my heart." He offered Randi his arm and she laid her hand on it.

Ahead of them John and Melody went slowly down

the great flight of stairs. The jubilant music throbbed in the air, which was scented by the massed daffodils.

They were at the drawing room door now, Randi was moving forward slowly on the lawyer's arm to where Jonas awaited her at the altar with the smiling clergyman and Cary, quiet and remote.

The beautiful words of the service were spoken, Jonas slipped the wedding ring on Randi's finger.

"I pronounce you man and wife."

There was a fractional pause and then Jonas held Randi lightly in his arms, brushed her cheek with his lips.

Then Melody had caught Randi in her arms, laughing and crying, and John followed, claiming a brother's right to kiss her. Cary withdrew beside the lawyer and, like the latter, shook hands with her and wished her well.

In the big formal dining room a buffet meal was presided over by a beaming Luther, who brought in an immense wedding cake and addressed Randi for the first time as Mrs. King.

The wedding ceremony took place at four o'clock. After that time seemed to be blurred. There were toasts and good wishes and congratulations. The servants came in as a group to offer their good wishes. Cary Hamilton was the first to leave, followed by the clergyman, and then by Billings.

Before going, Mr. Billings paused for a moment beside Jonas King. "I was wrong," he said. "She is a lovely person."

Jonas smiled. "I know," he agreed. "Very lovely."

At length John claimed Melody and took her away.
Then Jonas turned to smile at his young wife. "I
knew you would be a beautiful bride, my dear. Is everything — all right?"

"Just fine," she assured him gaily.

"What's that about John Lancing calling himself
your brother?"

"He and Melody are going to be married."

"Good heavens! It didn't take them long to fall in
love."

"No, it doesn't take long," Randi said quietly.

Kind eyes watched her. "Are you happy about it?"

She nodded emphatically. "Delighted. Melody loves
him and he loves her, and she will be wonderful for
little Andy, and she can live in Arizona where she will
keep well and strong. Anyhow, John is such a nice
person."

"Randi," Jonas asked, "have you any regrets? About
this marriage, I mean?"

Her brown eyes were steady and direct. "We are
going to make a good marriage of this," she assured
him.

"Yes." There was a pause. "I think we will, my
dear." He got up slowly. "And now, with your permis-
sion, I think I'll go to bed. Good night, Randi."

"Good night, Jonas. Sleep well."

"And at peace," he said. "Yes, I can do that, thanks
to you."

In the blue guest suite, Randi, with Sally's help, removed the cap with its short white veil. Odd, how heavy
it had felt. Slipped out of the white wedding dress, put

on the long white velvet housecoat with its matching slippers.

For a few minutes she sat before the mirror brushing her dark hair. She saw Sally watching her.

"That's all, Sally. I shan't want you again tonight."

"Yes, ma'am. Good night, Mrs. King." Sally smiled shyly and went out, closing the door behind her.

Absently Randi put down the hairbrush, switched out the lights, went to sit on the cushioned window seat looking out into the dark garden, out toward the guesthouse.

My wedding day, she thought. Such a strange, strange day. But Jonas is safe. That much I have achieved. Jonas is safe. And Melody is going to be happy.

My wedding night. And I am alone. More alone than I had realized one could be. She found her eyes going, against her will, toward the guesthouse with its lighted windows. I must not think of him. I must not think of him. Oh, Jonas, I am going to be a true wife, a loyal wife.

She dropped her face in her hands, unaware of the tears that trickled through her fingers. Then she raised her head, listening. There were sounds overhead. Someone seemed to be walking in the room above her, which should be unoccupied. She stood up, holding her breath, listening. And then in the dark garden she saw movements. Someone was going toward the guesthouse. She realized then that however much Hubert might hate his brother, he feared even more the man who was making a lifework of blocking him. Cary Hamilton.

Without pausing to think, Randi ran out of her room, down the stairs, pushed back the bolt on the front door.

ii

As Sally came out of Randi's suite and closed the door she heard the quiet feet on the stairs. Her heart was thudding. Miss Bertram must have come back! She opened the sitting room door and slipped back into the dark room, noticing that Miss Scott's — Mrs. King's — bedroom door was closed. From here she could see the man coming up the stairs, and she stared in disbelief. It was Hal Peters! Then she remembered that he had come here to live, he had a right to be in the house.

She let herself out of the sitting room and started up the stairs to her own room. Then she heard the sound of muffled voices, heard the footsteps. There were people on the third floor but not in Hal's room. She knew which his was because she had helped Mrs. Wilkes prepare it.

She hesitated for a moment and then rapped softly on Hal's door. He opened it and looked at her in surprise. Before he could speak she laid her finger on her lips.

"Something is wrong," she whispered urgently. "There is someone across the hall."

"It's all right," he assured her.

"You mean you aren't going to do anything?" She was incredulous.

He shook his head, smiling. "Go on to bed, Sally, and don't worry."

She ignored the smile. "If you won't do anything, I

will. I'm going to call the police. There has been enough trouble here."

"No," he said sharply, and then lowered his voice cautiously. "Go to bed and don't say anything."

She turned abruptly and started down the stairs. Before she had gone three steps, Hal had caught up with her. As she jerked free of his hand he took her by the shoulders, forced her to stop, holding her against him.

"I swear to you that everything is all right," he said, his voice just above a whisper.

"I don't believe you," she said dully. "I just don't believe you. Let go of me or I'll scream."

"And shock Mr. King into a heart attack?"

She slumped wearily, not knowing what to do. After a glance at her face, Hal took her arm and this time, unresisting, she went with him to the library on the second floor. He switched on lights, closed the door, nodded to one of the big comfortable chairs drawn up before the empty grate of the fireplace.

"All right," he said, "I'm going to tell you the truth." He smiled into the bitter, disillusioned eyes. "Really the truth this time. It's a long story, Sally, but I need your help, so —"

She gave him a cynical look, leaned back in her chair.

He started with the work of the All-American Party, with its appeal to bigots and neurotics, to the frustrated and semieducated, the people to whom violence seemed more possible, and certainly easier, than self-government. He explained why Jonas King had been in danger because his brother was determined to get hold of his money, how he himself had begun to work for John Lancing and had infiltrated the party, how Cary Hamilton had become the strongest force in the opposition.

Sally moved restlessly. She was not interested in politics. Hal smiled at her again and she almost found herself smiling back until she remembered how he had spoken of her to the state police lieutenant.

He went on to explain how Hubert had recruited youngsters from orphanages. At this she was more alert. He explained Mavis Bertram's role in getting hold of her.

"You are in the clear," he told her. "You are going to stay in the clear. There is nothing for you to fear for yourself any more."

She made no reply and did not look at him, her eyes on the empty grate.

"I didn't tell you these things before," he said, "because we hoped my position here need not come out. But the time for that has passed."

For the first time she really looked at him. There was no friendliness or trust in the bleak little face. "Something is going on right now in this house," she said, "and you are deliberately keeping me from knowing it."

"No," he said, "I am going to take a calculated risk. I am going to have faith in my opinion of you. I am going to trust you with the truth, knowing it is possible that you may betray us all to Hubert King."

She frowned. "I don't understand you."

"It's simple enough. Hubert wants to get rid of Cary

Hamilton and his friend Lancing. The sounds you heard upstairs were Hamilton and Lancing moving into this house for the night. I've been taking their place in the guesthouse during the day because, especially during the wedding, it would be easy for someone to get in there and set a booby trap of some sort. Tonight, a man from the state police has taken over and is out there on guard."

There was a long pause in the room. "Well?" Peters said at last gently.

"I won't say anything to anyone. No one could make me, even if they tortured me. I don't see why you thought I would."

He was beside her now, drawing her to her feet. He held one small cold hand closely in his warm one. "You didn't have faith in me. I was afraid perhaps you didn't have any more faith in anyone."

Her eyes were quite steady. "Since knowing Miss Scott — Mrs. King — I have learned to have faith in goodness. And I wouldn't ever betray — anyone." Her voice broke.

Somehow she found herself sobbing against his shoulder.

"Sally," he said gently. "Little Sally." His arms comforted her, holding her close. "You know something," he said, speaking into the soft hair that brushed his face, "I enjoyed every minute of that evening we had together. I —" As she stirred, tried to release herself, his hold grew firmer. "I didn't betray you to the police, little Sally. I was trying to clear you with them."

This time he let her stand back in the circle of his arms. She met his smiling eyes. "Next time," he said, "we'll go dancing. It would be fun to dance with you. Okay?"

She smiled back. "Okay," she promised.

He took her by the shoulders, gave her a little shove toward the door. "Now go up to bed and don't worry."

"What are you going to do?"

"Follow my own advice and get some sleep." He grinned at her. "Good night, Sally."

"Good night, Hal." She went swiftly up the stairs, aware of the muffled sounds from the two rooms on the third floor but no longer disturbed by them.

Hal looked after her, smiling. He turned to switch off the lights and looked out into the dark garden. There was the momentary gleam of a flashlight. Grant had not planned to patrol the grounds; he was to remain in the guesthouse. Peters moved softly down the stairs, fumbled with the lock on the front door. Someone, he realized in dismay, had left the bolt unfastened. For a moment he hesitated, uncertain whether he should alert Hamilton or the trooper. He decided on the latter, went out and closed the door behind him.

iii

When Cary returned to the guesthouse after the wedding, Peters, who had been reading, closed his book and smiled. "Did everything go off all right?"

Cary nodded grimly. "John has taken Melody home.

They'll probably go somewhere to dance so he will be late. Is everything quiet here?"

"Not a sound, not a movement."

"You might as well go back to the house," Cary said.

"If you don't mind, I'll stay here until Grant takes over. Those were his orders."

"As you like." Cary hunted for a pipe and a book and went upstairs, eager to be alone. He did not open the book, simply tossed it on a chair, and began to pace the room. Never again would he have to go through such an ordeal as he had today, seeing the girl he loved marry another man. True, it was not to be a real marriage; Jonas had made that clear to him. But the girl's vows were as binding, as final; they would be kept as loyally as though it were. He knew that. Even — no, he pushed away the thought of Willis Jameson. He did not believe Randi loved Willis Jameson. There was some other explanation. There had to be.

A door closed softly and there were muttered questions and answers. Cary stood listening. Then he heard Peters say, "Only Mr. Hamilton. Mr. Lancing isn't back yet. He was taking Miss Scott home, and perhaps to dance somewhere."

"I don't like that," Grant said sharply. "That's what I meant by a man in love being unreliable. I wanted them both right here under my eye. Well, there's nothing you can do here now. You might as well escort Mr. Hamilton back to the main house and get yourself some rest. I'll see that Lancing gets over safely as soon as he returns. Nothing to report, I suppose."

Peters was cheerful. "All quiet on the western front."

Peters called Cary and the two men said a low-voiced good night to Grant and made their way cautiously across the dark garden and into the house, using Peters's key. They went softly up the stairs to the third floor.

"Sorry about this," Peters said in a low voice, "but Grant doesn't want you to show a light in here. These rooms are supposed to be empty, you know."

Cary nodded. "All right. I'll make out."

He heard Peters go back to his own room across the hall and then he moved restlessly to the window. Having always been a man of action, he found it maddening to wait in the dark while another man took the risks, if there were any risks to be taken. At length he heard Peters go down the stairs to admit Lancing. In a few moments the latter tapped at his door and came in.

"You there, Cary?"

"By the window. They don't want us to show any lights."

Lancing groped his way over to his friend.

"Did you have a pleasant evening?"

"Wonderful, Cary! We went dancing. We're going to be married in a few weeks, as soon as Melody can get ready. We're going to Lake Louise for our honeymoon and then come back here. We'll live in her cottage until we return to Phoenix in the fall."

"I'm glad for you," Cary said. "Very glad. Melody is lovely and she'll be good for the boy."

"You know, Cary, Melody and I ran into rather a queer thing tonight and we thought we'd better tell you about —"

Cary stretched out his hand in the dark, found his friend's arm, his grip tightened on it. "What's that?"

Someone had tapped on Peter's door, there were whispers. Peters and someone else were going downstairs. Cary's hand relaxed. "This waiting around gets on my nerves, I guess," he apologized.

"Do you think Hubert will really try something?"

"I think," Cary said grimly, "he will have to. He knows I'll never give up as long as he is in that filthy racket. Only — I prefer to fight my own battles, not have someone else do it for me."

"But this," Lancing reminded him quietly, "isn't a private battle, Cary."

"That's true. Good night, John."

When Lancing had groped his way to the door and gone back to his own room, Cary returned to the window. He could not go to bed. He was waiting for something to happen though he did not know what it was. Someone came quietly up the stairs and he tensed. Then the feet went on to the fourth floor and a door closed softly.

He stared down into the garden, leaned forward with his forehead pressed against the windowpane. Down below a light flashed. A dark shadow moved where other shadows were still. Then there was a streak of white, a slim woman running. She had flung her arms around a man who seemed to be waiting for her.

"No," Cary groaned to himself. "Randi, how can you? How can you?"

Then the white figure was pitched across the path as though she had been flung there, and the man was running.

Cary threw open his door and raced down the stairs, pulled open the front door, pounded around the house toward the garden.

The powerful beam moved, caught the man who was racing around the house, a handsome young man with a long lock of hair falling across his forehead.

Then Grant's voice said sharply, "Hamilton! Call the barracks. I've got him. Better get hold of a doctor. Something has happened to the girl."

He moved the light, catching a boy with a straggly beard and fanatical eyes, a boy holding in his hand a fire bomb. And beyond, lying across the path in a white velvet housecoat, was Randi, her cheek darkening from a bruise, her eyes closed. For one anguished moment Cary knelt beside her, found her pulse. Then he lifted her in his arms and carried her into the guesthouse. He dialed the state police barracks and then called a doctor.

XIX

RANDI ran around the house, then more slowly along the dark path, because it was difficult to see, to avoid the bushes on either side that caught at the long velvet robe. She wished now that she had stopped to change, because white was so terribly visible; whether or not she could see, she could easily be seen. But she had had only one thought: Cary was in the guesthouse and he might be in danger.

Then a man stepped onto the path and she saw the glint of metal in his hands. She did not seem to think at all. She flung out her arms, catching at his sleeves, trying to make a bulwark of her own slim body.

Then an arm, unexpectedly muscular, pushed her away, knocked her so that she was falling across the path, dropping into darkness.

There were feet pounding along the gravel path, the beam of a high-powered flashlight struck Willis's face, as he stood, half paralyzed with shock and fear, his mouth opening and closing like fish out of water. Then someone shouted, "Hamilton! I've got him." And after that there was nothing at all.

When she opened her eyes it was to see the face of Jonas's doctor. He smiled at her.

"You're going to be all right. You'll have a bruise on your cheek for a while where you scraped it on the gravel, and probably a headache. You knocked your head when you fell, but I doubt if there is any concussion."

He spoke to someone whom Randi could not see. "How about Mr. King?"

"He is in the front guest suite at the house and never heard a thing. Sleeping like a baby. Peters just checked."

"And what was this young lady doing out in that dark garden?" For the first time the doctor seemed to notice the exquisite white velvet robe.

"She will probably be able to explain that to you later — to your satisfaction."

Surely that could not be Cary's voice, cold, contemptuous, the voice of an enemy. He sounded as though he hated her.

"Did they get the man who tried to bomb the guest-house?" the doctor asked.

"One of them." That was Lancing's voice. "The other one escaped."

The doctor nodded. "There is no reason why Mrs. King could not go back to the house, if she has a little help. She'll be all right after a night's sleep."

Randi realized then that she was in the living room of the guesthouse with Cary, John, and the physician. The latter, after a long, curious look at her, nodded, picked up his small black bag, and went wearily out of the room.

Randi tried to sit up; for a moment the room revolved dizzily, and then steadied.

"Better take it easy," John warned her.

"What happened?" she demanded. "What happened?"

"Don't worry," Cary told her harshly, "he got away. Thanks to you. That was quick thinking, running interference for him."

Her eyes were wide with shock, almost blank as she stared at him without understanding.

It was Lancing who, seeing her expression, gave a sharp exclamation. "Take it easy, Cary! You're on the wrong track. I think we have both been on the wrong track."

"Not any more," Cary said. "I'm cured."

"Will you, or will you not, let me speak my piece?"

"Oh, sure. Sure." Cary lighted his pipe, taking his time, went to stare out into the dark garden, which was peaceful now, where no shadows moved.

"All right, then get a load of this. I started to tell you about the queer thing Melody and I ran into when we went dancing tonight — last night. It's nearly four o'clock now. Anyhow, I took her to Sands Roadhouse, because that's the only place within thirty miles of here where you can dance. There weren't many people there, three or four teen-age couples, a few older couples, and a guy with a bee-utiful blonde. What I noticed first was the woman's looks. Then her emerald ring. And then

Melody told me that the man was Willis Jameson, who had been engaged to Randi for a long time. He was so engrossed in his blonde that he never even noticed us."

Randi was sitting upright now, her eyes on Cary's averted face. John Lancing looked down at her, tried to catch her eye, to smile encouragingly, but she was almost unaware of his presence.

"According to Melody," John went on, "Randi was engaged to this guy for a long time. She's a — trusting and loyal sort of girl. She believed in him when no one else did. Certainly not Melody. Anyhow, when Mr. King asked Randi to marry him she refused him without a moment's hesitation because of Jameson. She wasn't interested in the money or in what he could offer her. She just wanted her salary to help make things easier for Melody — and for Jameson.

"Then she went to our hero's office to meet him and found him with a gorgeous blonde, probably the one he was with last night, and she discovered for herself what sort of heel he is. When she finally accepted Jonas it was, according to Melody, because she had lost faith in love but not faith in mankind. She realized that by marrying Jonas she could help protect him from his brother, help prolong his life. And, of course, she wasn't concerned about all that money because she understood that it was to go to you, a thing, by the way, of which she heartily approved."

Cary was standing rigid, the pipe in his hand was cold.

"Well, Willis Jameson made a couple of attempts to

persuade Randi to break with Jonas, and then he gave up. Tonight, when Melody and I saw him with his blonde, the girl was arguing with him. I got a feeling that, in her own way, she probably loves the guy, though she has no illusions about him." Lancing repeated the conversation he had overheard:

"Willis, you've got to get away. Hubert intends to involve you. I saw it in his face. Go away now. Let's go together. Let Manton carry on alone."

"I've got to obey orders, at least this once more."

"You're afraid of him, aren't you?"

"Okay, so I'm afraid. But there's no escaping him. I'll see this business through tonight and then —"

"It will be too late." The girl was nearly crying.

"Anyhow, I need the money. I've got to have the money. Unless you will sell that emerald."

"I'd do almost anything for you, darling. Almost. Not that."

"Poor Willis," Randi commented. "So weak. So —"

Cary turned and their eyes met across the room. After a long moment she flung up her hand as though to thrust away something intolerable. "Oh, no!" she cried.

"Look here, Cary," John told him. "You still don't see it. Hubert sent Manton and Willis Jameson tonight to bomb the guesthouse. Or rather, so far as I can make out, Manton was to do the work but Jameson was to be so involved that he'd be unable to clear himself. Randi wasn't running interference for Jameson, as you appear to think. She was — I'd be willing to take my oath —

running to warn us, to save us. To save you. She might have blown herself up. It's a miracle she didn't. Didn't you see the way she tried to use her own body as a shield between the house and the bomb?"

"Randi!" It was a cry of torture as Cary came toward her.

Randi held out a shaking hand as though to ward him off. "It doesn't really matter," she said, her voice a thread, her face white and still. "John, will you help me go back — home?"

With John Lancing's arm firm around her, supporting her, she went toward the big house, went without a backward look.

ii

Cary was pacing the floor when John came back.

"Peters called Sally, and the girl is putting Randi to bed," John reported. "She'll be all right." Seeing Cary's expression, he said, "Everything will be all right."

Cary laughed shortly. "Nothing will be all right. Like a fool, a blind fool, a jealous fool, I've smashed everything."

John was too honest, too true a friend to deny it. "Jealousy is the very devil," he agreed. "It blinds people, warps judgment, causes unnecessary pain. Well, that's water over the dam now."

"What am I going to do, John?"

John looked at him sharply. "Well," he said without sympathy, "if you are able to stop thinking of yourself and being sorry for yourself for a minute, there's a lot you can do. You have a big stake in the game of destroying the All-American Party, or have you forgotten that?"

"No, I haven't forgotten."

"What I am thinking of now isn't Hubert King and his sordid little power drive. I'm thinking of his victims." As Cary started to speak he went on quickly, "I don't mean you and me, because he tried to have us killed last night. I'm thinking of young Manton, the boy he took out of an orphanage, whom he brainwashed, whom he has turned into a tool. The kid isn't bad, Cary, he's simply misled. He thinks he is helping a great cause and he is willing to take any risk for it. Boys like Manton can be allowed to become criminals or they can be salvaged."

"Well?"

"Let's go to the police barracks," John suggested. "You have always been able to stir the imagination of the young. Why not see what you can do for Manton?"

The two men exchanged looks. Then Cary smiled. "Thanks, John," he said simply.

When they entered the state police barracks, Lieutenant Barker and young Grant were talking to the Manton boy. A sullen boy. Having been caught with a bomb, he felt like a hero. Now, as might be expected in his world, the brutal police were going to be cruel to him. There was a mocking look in the fanatical eyes, and a sneer distorted the weak mouth with its scraggly beard.

All three looked up as the two men came in.

"Any luck?" Lancing asked.

Barker glared at the silent boy. "Not a word out of him." He added, "So far," and Manton laughed tauntingly.

"What!" Cary said. "No rubber hose? No thumb-screws?"

"What about Jameson and the Bertram woman?" Lancing asked, and the boy was more alert, his eyes moving from face to face.

"They got away. They are leaving Manton to hold the bag. As you might expect. Not a trace of them. Jameson had cleared out of his office; his apartment has no clothes or personal possessions in it. A clean sweep. The girl has vanished too."

"Well," Cary laughed, "perhaps, after all, she agreed to sell her emerald ring and keep Jameson the way he'd like to be kept."

Manton started to protest and bit back the words.

Cary sat down facing him. "Look here, Manton," he said easily, in a man to man tone, "let's get the facts out in the open, shall we? That's the American way. But that's not the method of the All-American Party." He held up his hand. "No," he said as Manton started to argue, "you're going to hear some truth for once in your life. The group that calls itself All-American is a Fascist group that works underground, that picks its tools and trains them and lies to them. It doesn't work by honest debate and argument because it can't. It works by suggestion and lies and arousing hatred. And especially — it works by violence.

"Violence is always stupid. It is an indication that

self-government has failed. It's easy to throw a bomb. It's hard to arrive at an opinion for yourself. You aren't doing your own thinking, Manton. You are just expressing what Hubert King tells you.

"Now let's take a look at Hubert King. He's fairly typical of the men who head rackets like this. He forged a check at twenty-five; he never tried to hold a job in his life because he thought there must be an easier way of getting a living than by earning it. His father knew he was not to be trusted either with money or power, but he left him a generous income, bigger than most men work hard to get.

"But that wasn't enough for Hubert. He wanted his brother's money to buy importance and power for himself. So he has tried over and over to shock his brother into a heart attack so he would die. This is the truth, Manton. This is the man whom you have accepted as a leader. A criminal. A would-be assassin. But not brave enough to do his killing himself.

"He chose people like you, ignorant people who thought they were smart, to throw his bombs for him, to cut ropes so that harmless workmen and helpless girls might die. He chose people like you to stir up discontent and head demonstrations, because he realizes you haven't had enough history to recognize where these things lead, where they have always led.

"In recent years, with the world technically at peace, do you know how many wars there have been? Something like twenty-five! And no one knows how many of them have been started simply because a demonstration got out of hand and led to violence: one death led to retaliation and then to a snowballing of violence with no one knowing exactly how it had come about or how to stop it."

Beyond ordering coffee, neither of the state troopers had spoken. Cary accepted a cup of coffee and gestured for one to be given to Manton. He sipped his own in a leisurely way. Manton looked at his as though suspecting that it contained some hidden poison before he ventured to taste it.

"Bombs in the night," Cary went on, "hurled at sleeping people; crashing scaffolds that might destroy the innocent. Violence, furtive and hidden. Nothing good has ever come of violence, Manton. We made America by building, not by destroying. Up to this point you haven't been a hero, just a small-time hoodlum used by a phony Grade B dictator."

He held Manton's eyes now, eyes that were defiant, that wavered, that were ashamed, that began slowly to reflect uncertainty.

Cary stood up. "For my money, you are a victim who thought he saw a splendid dream and did not look at the rotten reality. If you could risk so much for violence, how much would you be willing to risk to start over, to learn the excitement and fulfillment of building?"

Now there was a doubtful hope in Manton's eyes.

Cary turned to Barker. "I don't know just what charges will be laid against this kid, Lieutenant. That's out of my province. But I do ask this: when it is possible, I would like to have him paroled in my custody. Okay?"

"I think it could be arranged," Barker said, "and I must say, Mr. Hamilton, that considering the attempt that was made upon your life —"

Cary stopped him with a gesture. He looked at Manton, a question in his face.

"Okay," Manton said. Then his face lighted, became eager. "Gee — okay!"

XX

DAFFODILS gave way to apple blossoms, then laurel bloomed on the hills, and finally white fences were a glory of climbing red roses. The pale green of new leaves had become the full glory of great trees in all their splendid panoply of midsummer. There was the mammoth rugged oak tree under which George Washington had once held an impromptu conference with his staff; there were wineglass elms that still survived the plague that had destroyed so many of their species; there were sugar maples casting deep shade over the velvet lawn.

The season that had brought such changes to the countryside had brought similar changes within the King house. Some of the heavy furniture had been replaced; dark draperies had given way to light ones; upholstery that had been gloomy now was bright and gay. Sunlight flooded the rooms of the house.

Jonas King walked with a lighter step and his health was better than it had been in many months. His deep cheerful laugh rang through the rooms. He devoted his mornings to working on his book. Peters, who had taken the job merely as an excuse to guard Jonas, found himself increasingly interested and involved in the work.

One day when he and Jonas had worked for several hours in deep concentration, Jonas leaned back to rest briefly.

"I begin to understand," Peters said, "the meaning of that phrase, 'The pen is mightier than the sword.' Perhaps there can be more achieved by a book like this than by dozens of acts of violence."

"I certainly hope so." Jonas studied the young man thoughtfully. "I have notes for other books," he said. "Notes I've been gathering for years. Lately, as you have probably noticed," and he smiled at his secretary, "I've asked you to rough out a draft for a chapter now and then. I have a feeling, Peters, that you could carry on when the pen gets too heavy for me to hold. Would you care to?"

"Surely you need not ask, Mr. King! It would be a trust, which I would do my best to carry out."

"Good. I must talk to Randi about it; explain that you are to carry on with this work, have my notes, and whatever material there is around. Where is she?"

"Last I saw of her" Peters said, "she was making the final arrangements for the garden party tomorrow."

Jonas smiled. "She never stops working, does she?" He looked toward the door with a smile. "Here you are, my dear. You're looking very bonny."

"Thank you, kind sir." Randi dropped a curtsy, laughing at the absurd figure she cut in her trim brown slacks and yellow sleeveless blouse. Her skin had tanned to a golden shade. She waved the two men back to their chairs and perched on the edge of the desk, clasped her hands around one knee and then looked in horror at her nails. "Heavens, I must find time for a manicure before tomorrow."

"You don't really need to grub in the dirt, you know," Jonas reminded her, laughing.

"I love it. And, oh, Jonas, the grounds do look so lovely. I'll keep my fingers crossed for sunshine. It would be such a pity to have to move everything indoors: the refreshment table and all that. And," she frowned, "of course, there is that fortune-telling tent."

"You know," Jonas said, "I think we're going to have to ask Peters to give up the garden party and act as a kind of monitor at that tent."

"What's that?" Peters asked alertly.

"Perhaps nothing at all," Jonas said. "Perhaps trouble. I honestly don't know and there's always a chance I've made a bad mistake."

Peters looked from one to the other. Jonas glanced at Randi.

"Well," she explained, "it's like this. A week ago, Hubert came to pay a belated wedding visit, to offer congratulations and all that. He was quite jovial. Anyone who didn't know about him would have believed he was delighted with our marriage. He paid me all sorts of compliments. It was a very strange situation. Then —"

What had happened was that Randi had felt obliged to ask him to the garden party at which she was to repay the hospitality she had received since her marriage.

"I just couldn't get out of it," she said, "when he was behaving as though he was so pleased about Jonas marrying me. Even though we knew — well, anyhow, the very next day he called up to say that, as he had not sent us a wedding present, he wanted to do something to please us and he was going to arrange to have a famous fortune-teller come to the garden party and entertain the guests, because people always love having their fortunes told, even when they don't believe a word of it. And I just didn't know how to prevent it. Only I don't like it one single bit. Hubert can't have changed that much."

"What amuses me," Jonas said, "is that Hubert must have learned by now that Sally is loyal to my wife. He must know that young Manton has become Hamilton's most devoted follower, that you have dropped out of the party, Peters, as quickly as you entered it. The situation is ludicrous in a way. Either he is reformed or he is trying to retrieve his position with his party by some now move. Or — he won't be satisfied until he has made me suffer for thwarting him."

"Have you told Cary about this?" Peters asked.

"No," Randi said carelessly. "He has been so busy, you know, on his lecture tours, that he isn't often here and I didn't feel that we should disturb him when he has so much on his mind. You know, he'll be leaving for California after the garden party."

"Just the same, I think he should be told," Peters said. "After all, he is deeply concerned in all this."

"I agree with you," Jonas said. "Of course, Lancing will be back tomorrow with Melody from their honeymoon. Between them —" Jonas smiled as he saw Peters's expression and corrected himself — "among the three of you everything should be under control. But don't trust Hubert too far. What's the Latin for it: *Timeo Danaos —*"

"I fear the Greeks, even when bringing gifts." Peters nodded. "We'll keep an eye both on Mr. Hubert and his fortune-teller. You know sir," he grinned, "instead of the fortune-teller having news for us it's just possible we'll have news for him."

ii

That afternoon, Randi went over the grounds for a last check. There were white garden chairs scattered over the grass; a few gay canopies stretched to provide shade in spots that were too exposed to the sun; the long refreshment table was ready, and there were extra people in the kitchen preparing for the elaborate buffet. The dance floor that had been constructed had been tested to make sure that it was solid and even, and now it was being carefully waxed. Randi had hired the best name band she could get for two hours of dancing, and a quartet that was to play earlier in the afternoon.

She looked with foreboding at the fortune-telling tent, but remembered that Hal Peters would be on guard.

She had been hurrying all day, checking off items on her list, making sure that no one had been left out of the invitation list, making sure that no detail had been neglected, that the buffet was under control, the music and chairs, the platform and canopies all prepared.

Now she sank wearily onto a long deck chair, lying in the sun, her eyes moving from a great maple tree to the deep shade it cast, on to bright sunlight on green lawn, and beyond to the rose garden with its magnificent beds of prize rosebushes, which at the peak of their bloom were scenting the air. Jonas had told her, only the day before, that the garden had never been so lovely, nor the house so bright, nor his heart so light. As he had foretold, she had brought sunlight.

As she moved idly, the sun reflected in a dozen facets from the diamond on her finger. It no longer troubled her. She watched the rainbow hues dazzle from the ring without unhappiness. Of course, she thought, she was not unhappy. She had made Jonas's home bright for him, had made life safe and even gay for him, she had seen Melody married to the man she loved and knew that she would be beloved and secure and taken care of. What then had Randi to regret? That her life was empty and meaningless? This would not be true. It was filled with activity, with affection and trust. She was creating, in her own small way, a more beautiful world around her.

Love? Well, she had dreamed twice of love. Once when she had been attracted by Willis's boyish charm; the second time, and how differently, when she had first met Cary Hamilton, when he had looked at her, when his hand had closed on hers. There had been that poignant moment at Tiffany's when he had slipped the ring on her finger and she had thought, in mingled consternation and delight, *This is my real marriage.*

And then there had been the moment when she had raced through a dark garden to save his life, had tried to hurl herself between the bomb and the guesthouse, and Cary, cold, contemptuous, disillusioned, had believed that she had come, on the night of her wedding, for an infamous secret meeting with Willis Jameson.

Perhaps, Randi thought, staring up into the blue vault of the sky, it had been better to have love die in her like that. Better than carrying unendurable pain around with her. Now she was free. She had only one purpose now, to keep Jonas happy and well. And tomorrow she would see Melody again. Melody radiant from her honeymoon.

Melody and John were to spend the night in the main house, and tomorrow, after Cary left for California, left forever, they would move into the guesthouse. And then, in a few months, Melody too would be gone, gone a long, long way. More than two thousand miles. But that didn't really matter as long as she was happy.

In a way, Randi realized, it was going to be more painful to part with Andy than with Melody. The sisters would correspond, they would meet frequently. But Andy — for the past weeks Randi had taken care of him, come to love the enchanting small boy. It would be a wrench to lose him. How wonderful it would be to have a child of her own!

Randi found her eyes resting on the guesthouse.

How careful Cary had been to avoid her! Nearly three months had passed during which they had encountered each other barely half a dozen times. He had been wise, she thought. She glanced at her watch. Time to go back and change for dinner. Afterwards she would read to Jonas. A tranquil, happy evening. And tomorrow she would take her place for the first time publicly as Mrs. Jonas King.

iii

"Randi!" someone exclaimed. "How lovely she is, Jonas. No wonder you have kept her to yourself."

For an hour Jonas's old friends and neighbors had been greeting Randi with warmth and neighborliness, in spite of their surprise over her youth.

Beside her, Jonas beamed, welcomed friends, presented his wife proudly, accepted compliments and good wishes.

"It's going well, isn't it?" Randi asked him, during a moment's respite on the receiving line.

"Beautifully." Jonas looked at the crowd scattered across the lawn, in twos and threes and small groups, heard the quartet playing on the platform where, in a few minutes, the dance band was to take its place, heard laughter, enjoyed the sound of the music, the heat of the sun on his bare head. But most of all he enjoyed the sight of his young wife, in a white chiffon dress, her dark hair shining in the sun, the uptilted brows clearly etched above the brown eyes, skin glowing from her hours in the garden.

"But I knew you would handle it beautifully, my dear. You've never disappointed me. Not once." His eyes smiled at her as well as his lips.

"Here, here," said a laughing voice, "husbands and wives are not supposed to be together at a party."

Jonas laughed too. "A fine one you are to say that," he said to John Lancing, who held Melody's arm linked with his. The bride and groom looked radiant with happiness.

Randi's heart sang as she looked at her sister. Where once life had flickered like a candle in a breeze, it glowed now, steady and warm.

"We're going to have our fortunes told," John said with a quick look at Randi, who returned the look with a question in her eyes. "Peters seems to be hanging around the tent in an oddly suspicious sort of way."

"Have you seen Hu —" Randi broke off.

"Our beautiful bride," Hubert said in his bland voice. Pudgy hands closed over her bare arms, he gave her a smacking kiss on the cheek. "Jonas, you are a lucky devil."

The quartet had taken its departure and the band at the end of the dance platform began to play.

Hubert looked around in surprise. "Oh, I didn't know there was to be dancing."

So that's it, Randi thought, her nerves tingling in alarm. The fortune-telling tent was to provide a diversion, to distract attention from — well, from what? Something is wrong.

"My dear," Jonas said, "I think you should lead the

dancing. Sorry I can't —" He turned. "There you are, Cary. Just in the nick of time. You've become almost a stranger. Will you and Randi lead the dancing?"

There was a fractional hesitation and then Cary, tall and distinguished in his white jacket, held out his hand. "Will you?"

As they stepped onto the platform Randi said, oddly breathless, to prevent silence lengthening between them, "There are to be two kinds of music. The kind the kids like and more conservative music for Jonas's generation. This —"

The orchestra was playing, "I'll Follow My Secret Heart," and Cary took her in his arms, a slim girl with dark hair and a dress like a white cloud, and swung her across the polished platform in the waltz.

They danced in complete silence for one minute, for two. Then a second couple and a third followed them.

"For three months," Cary said at last, "I've wanted to say, 'I'm sorry, Randi.' Sorrier than there are words to tell you. But I — waited. And now I can't wait any longer. I'm going away tonight. This is good-by. But can you find it in your heart to forgive me for the terrible injustice I did you?"

She stepped, turned, moved in his arms almost as though they were one person. At last she raised her eyes to find him watching her face with a kind of hopeless longing.

"It's all right, Cary," she told him. She was afraid of her revealing eyes, her joy in his presence. "Listen," she said quickly, "I think something is wrong." She explained about the fortune-telling tent. "Hubert wanted to keep people interested. He didn't know about the dancing so he set this up for something. Hal Peters is watching the tent, but I don't think the danger is there."

"Danger? But that's all over now surely. Anyhow, young Manton is going to watch — your husband, to protect him." He broke off as a hand touched his shoulder, a man stepped forward, took Randi from him, continued the step without a break.

"Darling," Willis said, "you're lovelier than you ever were."

She stared at him in disbelief. Then she tried to draw away, found herself firmly held. Only by making a scene could she escape from him. "Let me go at once," she said, her voice low and furious. "At once!"

Through the crowd she saw Melody staring at her, saw her turn in search of John, saw John disappearing inside the fortune-telling tent.

"Never again," Willis said exultantly. "You are going to be mine, my precious. Remember I told you once that all roads lead to Rome."

"I remember." Randi's voice was icy, contemptuous. "I have married a rich man. So you believe, you honestly believe, I'll turn to you, let you live out the rest of your life on Jonas's money."

He laughed down at her. "I honestly do."

"Where have you been hiding?" she asked.

Something in her tone cut through his conceit, his assurance that she was his for the taking. "Hiding?" He was at a loss.

"After you tried to murder John and Cary."

"Murder! My dearest girl, you sound mad!" He laughed, but his laughter was lacking in confidence, oddly uneasy.

"No, I'm very sane, Willis. I wonder you dare come here. Do you think we aren't protecting Jonas? Do you think we aren't watching the — fortune-teller?" Randi herself did not know what had made her say it, but she watched the shock grow in his face.

"The Gypsy?" He spoke as though puzzled, but there was shock in his voice too.

"I don't know. Is it a Gypsy? I haven't seen the fortune-teller myself. All I know is that Hubert arranged to provide the tent and the performer, whoever it is."

Willis moved with his usual grace. He had always been a superb dancer. He looked very white, though by midsummer he was usually brown from swimming and tennis. He looked, Randi thought, as though he had literally been underground.

"Willis," she said, and he looked down at her, caught the urgency in her voice, "you have only one chance. You are finished here. Hubert is finished. Whatever he is involved in will inevitably involve you. You must go away, start over somewhere else. Try to build a decent life."

"When we marry —"

"We will never marry, Willis. Never. Even if — if anything happened to Jonas, especially if anything happened to Jonas. Get that idea out of your mind forever. But go while you can. I can almost feel the trap closing in on you."

"If you feel all that it must be because you love me."

She shook her head. Her eyes were sad. "Because you are — lost."

"My dance, I think." John Lancing tapped Willis's shoulder and the latter was obliged to step back. A moment later he mingled with the crowd, disappeared in it.

"Oh, thank goodness!" Randi exclaimed.

"Melody got to me as soon as she saw what had happened. What did he want?"

"He said he wanted to marry me when — Jonas —"

"Why, the — the —"

"John, I saw you go into the fortune-telling tent. What is happening in there?"

"The usual Gypsy. Cross-my-palm-with-silver deal. Long black hair, dark skin. Only the fool woman couldn't bear to remove that emerald ring."

"Mavis Bertram!"

Lancing nodded. "The same. I tipped off Peters, who swears he won't let her out of sight. She has a line waiting to get in now. Hubert is masterminding the deal, hauling in the crowd."

Cary had cut in again. He spoke quietly to John, who nodded and hurried off the platform. Cary looked down at Randi, saw her alarmed eyes.

"What is it?" she demanded. "Hubert is up to something." She looked out from the raised platform across the garden. "Where is Hubert? Where is Jonas? Come on, Cary."

She caught his hand and ran from the platform, ran through the crowd, threading her way, apologizing, paying no attention to the laughing remarks called to her, searching for Jonas.

"Where is he?" she demanded. "What is happening to him?"

Cary looked over her shoulder. "I can't see him in the garden."

Randi raced toward the front door, asked a breathless question of Luther.

"Mr. King? He went upstairs a few minutes ago, madam."

She was on the stairs now with Cary close behind her. Then he caught her arm, held her still.

"Still trying, Hubert?" That was Jonas. "There's nothing to gain now. No one under heaven could break my will as it is set up. Nothing to gain."

"You've taken everything," Hubert said. "Everything. The house. The money. My future. Even the people I trusted and who believed in me and the party — you've taken them too."

"You have enough money to live well, happily. What more do you want?"

"You've taken what I wanted. Now I'm going to see you don't get anything out of it. Anything more."

There was a sudden movement, a stifled cry from Jonas, and then young Manton said savagely, "Oh, no, you don't!" He reached Hubert, who was standing over his brother, and knocked him out with one swift jab on the jaw.

Randi had wrenched away from Cary's restraining hand, she was running up the last few stairs, across the hallway and into the library. Young Manton stood looking down at an unconscious Hubert. Jonas, one hand clawing at his chest, saw Randi at the doorway, he smiled at her in love and trust, and pitched onto the floor.

XXI

WITH Jonas's heart attack the garden party came to an abrupt end. The young Lancings, white-faced and horrified, went among the guests to explain that their host had collapsed and to receive their words of sympathy as they took their leave.

"What happened? What happened?" The question was repeated over and over, but no one seemed to know the answer. It was not until the newscasts of the following day that some part of the truth came out.

Jonas King's brother had been caught in an attempt to injure him, and Jonas had died of the shock. Young Mrs. King, who had been hostess at the season's most memorable garden party, was in seclusion. Hubert King and his attorney Willis Jameson, whom he accused of being responsible for the plot, were under arrest. Hubert was not talking. Willis Jameson had been persuaded to talk.

There was one point on which the newscasters had not been informed. Mavis Bertram had slipped through the net and disappeared.

Randi, supported by John and Melody, attended the private services for Jonas and then, in spite of Cary's protests that she remain at the King house, returned to her old cottage. Next day, Cary left for the coast.

Through the long summer that followed, Randi had the constant and loving support of Melody and John, who were staying at the guesthouse.

"But what," Melody asked anxiously, "are you planning to do, Randi? Jonas would not have wanted you to shut yourself away like this."

"I don't know," Randi said honestly. "I'm just — waiting."

Both Hubert and Willis were out on bail, as their cases would not come up for trial until the fall term. Once Randi came face to face with Willis on the street and was shocked by the change in him. He seemed to have aged without growing up. For a long moment they looked at each other and then she turned away, ignoring his cry of, "Randi!"

Mrs. Echo had found other employment when Melody married, so Randi asked Sally to take her place at the cottage, as she no longer had a job at the big house.

"I won't need a personal maid but I do want someone to do the housework and some cooking."

"I've never tried," Sally admitted, "but I would like to learn."

"There's nothing like practice. Anyhow," and Randi smiled, "one of these days you may find it important to run a house. You may as well practice on me."

Color deepened in Sally's face and she agreed without further demur.

Hal Peters had taken over the script of Jonas's

unfinished book and the notes he had made for future volumes. On the ample allowance Jonas had left Randi, she was able to pay him an adequate salary. And he was, she suggested, to continue to have his rooms in the big house. Cary would want him to have them, at least until he returned to establish his own residence there.

Peters thought about it for some time. "All right," he said at last, "I'll do it, but I'm not going to take credit for this book. Most of the work is Mr. King's. I'd like it to be a memorial to him."

"That's wonderful!" Randi exclaimed, tears in her eyes. "The kind of memorial he would like best."

So during the long summer, Peters worked on the book, finished it, and sent it off to a publisher. More and more, he had developed a habit of calling for Sally in the evenings, taking her to a movie, for a drive, or to dance somewhere. She was an easy girl to be with, easy to entertain, easily pleased, flatteringly interested in what he had to tell her. And she made no demands on him. She was also the kind of girl who watched the right-hand side of the menu and tried to order inexpensively to save his pocket.

One night, when Randi was to have dinner with John and Melody, she said, "Why don't you ask Hal to dinner tonight? Show him what a good cook you have become." Something of the old Randi, lighthearted and mischievous, flashed in the wide brown eyes.

"Oh, Mrs. King! Gee, thanks, I'd love to. What shall I cook?"

"What does he like most?"

"Roast beef and mashed potatoes and green beans and apple pie," Sally said promptly. "I notice whenever he has just been paid that's what he orders. Then, of course, it gets down to hamburg and frankfurters toward the end of the month."

Randi laughed. "A roast of beef it is."

So when Hal parked his shabby car in front of the cottage at seven o'clock, Sally called, "I'm in the kitchen!" She was bustling around, basting the roast, whose appetizing smell made Hal say, "Ah!" in a pleased way. She straightened up from the oven, her face flushed, her hair pushed back carelessly.

For a long moment Hal stood staring at her in amazement. For heaven's sake, he thought, this is the girl I want to marry! This is the one I want to come home to all the rest of my life. Why didn't I ever guess that before?

Sally closed the oven door and straightened up. "I just have to make the gravy and mash the potatoes and we'll be all ready."

"There's no hurry," Hal told her in an odd voice.

"No —" She looked at him and her voice seemed to catch in her throat, which was suddenly dry. "I'll see if the water pitcher is filled," she began breathlessly.

"I'll take care of that." He put his hands on her shoulders. "Sally?"

"Yes?"

"Look at me."

She looked up into his face and saw his expression.

He nodded to her. "Yes, it's like that, Sally. I want

to marry you. Do you think you could put up with me for a long time — say like always?"

Her hands were on his chest, holding him away while she searched his face. "I wish —"

The words were stifled against his chest as he drew her to him. Then he released her. "What do you wish?"

She laughed up at him, her face gay and confident. For the first time in her life she believed in her world and found it good.

"I wish," she said, "there was a longer word than always."

ii

Summer blazed with the scorching heat of August, and September brought cool nights and autumn flowers. Then in October came the spectacular burst of glory that makes New England for two or three weeks one of the most magnificent beauty spots in the world. There was real warmth only at noon now, with cool afternoons and sometimes touches of frost in the morning.

Then after a night of high wind Randi awakened to see the trees stripped of their leaves, the branches standing stark against the sky. The time of blossoming had gone, the time of the long winter sleep had come. Months would have to pass, months of bone-breaking cold, of snow and ice, before the earth would bloom again.

Randi, staring out at the bare trees, felt desolate as

she had never been before. John and Melody had taken
Andy to Phoenix for the winter. A letter from Cary
had offered the guesthouse to Peters and Sally as at
least a temporary home. Cary had written from California, his letter addressed to Hal Peters, who showed
it to Randi.

"What a guy!" he exclaimed. "What a grand guy!"

Cary had enclosed his check for one hundred dollars
as a wedding present and congratulated Peters on the
fine work he had done in completing Jonas King's
book. "He would be proud of you. Good luck to it. I'll
see you in the spring."

That was the part of the letter that Randi remembered. *I'll see you in the spring.* It was all she had heard
of him since he had gone away after Jonas's funeral. He
had urged her to stay at the house but she had refused.
It was his house, she reminded him. She couldn't
remain there.

Cary was gone and Melody was gone and the summer was gone, and Jonas, whose last thought had been
to smile at her, to show his faith and trust in her.

Thanksgiving came and Christmas and New Year's,
days that in the past had been times of rejoicing, that
were now times of waiting. Randi never asked herself
for what she waited.

There was one unhappy period when, for several
days, she had to testify in court against Hubert King
and Willis. She felt no compunction about Hubert, but
she was glad when Willis, probably because of the
presence of impressionable women on the jury, got a

suspended sentence. Not that it really mattered. Willis, who had had nothing but vanity, had lost his faith in himself and his charm. He had nothing left.

Nothing? The day the trial ended Randi walked wearily out of court beside Billings. "We have Hubert sewed up for a good long time," he said in satisfaction, "but we let Willis Jameson slip through our fingers. Too bad."

Randi stopped to draw the collar of her coat up higher around her throat because of the raw, damp air. She saw Willis leaving the courthouse, jerking on dark glasses, saw him start aimlessly along the street, heard the tap of a horn.

He stopped short in disbelief. "Willis," said the husky contralto.

She was sitting at the wheel of an old car, her blond hair uncovered in spite of the raw air. She held out her hand from which she had stripped her driving glove.

Willis walked toward her slowly. "Mavis!" His face hardened. "What are you doing here?"

"There wasn't any point in showing up earlier. We couldn't help each other. It wouldn't have done you any good if I'd been caught too. But now —" The hand was still stretched out toward him.

"Now?" Willis said, unmoving.

"Look, you dope! I sold it. The emerald. I got this old heap and there's enough left to give us a start somewhere else. Maybe in the Middle West; maybe in the South. A new start."

"Mavis!"

She laughed, moved over into the passenger's seat. "From now on," she said, "you're in the driver's seat."

"Well, I'll be —" Billings exploded wrathfully.

"No, no, let them go," Randi pleaded. "If she cared that much, and she was always the stronger one, he has a chance still. They both may have a chance."

Billings's wrath faded as he looked down at her glowing face. "Every day I realize more and more how wise Jonas King was. You're quite a person, Randi King."

iii

The letter came from Melody late in March. Now March is a confusing month in New England. There are still heaps of dirty snow whose white has been drifted over by sand from trucks that are keeping the roads clear. There is deep mud. There can be winds that are bitter and penetrating. There can also be unexpected days when the sun is almost warm, when snowdrops and crocuses appear like stars on the ground, thrusting their fragile heads through the hard earth. And when the lakes and ponds are free of ice the voice of the peepers is heard, the first tangible evidence of renewal, of the resurrection of the earth, the first herald of spring.

That day Randi got a thicker letter than usual from Melody. Aside from her usual bundle of news, the work John was doing, and how adorable Andy was, and an ecstatic description of a trip they had made through Oak Creek Canyon — "We think the autumn is beautiful in New England. You should see this. It's always beautiful. The earth and the rocks and the mountains a brilliant red you can't imagine!" — there was, as usual, her most important news in a postscript.

"John and I are planning to come back by the first of May to spend the summer in the East. May we use the cottage?"

Randi sat frowning, wondering how three more people could fit into the cottage, which had only two bedrooms. They would work something out, of course. If necessary she could sleep on the couch in the living room.

Then, as she started to return the letter to its envelope, she noticed the smaller envelope inside and drew it out. There was her name in Jonas's writing, and below it Melody's headlong scrawl: "He gave me this the first night I met him. He said you were to have it when he could no longer speak for himself. Incredible as it seems, I'm afraid I forgot about it until just now."

"My Beloved Randi," the letter began, "you are to receive this only when I am gone, so I can speak to you without hesitation or restraint. Perhaps you will have wondered many times why I allowed you to marry me, knowing that I could only cause you a great deal of pain. I am not blind, my dear. I know that you and Cary love each other. I know that as well as I know that you will both be loyal to me.

"I would not have put you in this position if it had

seemed to me that individual happiness, even yours, comes first. But I don't believe that. At this point something evil is happening and it must be stopped. If Hubert has a clear field, the extent of that evil will be increased tenfold. The only way I know to prevent that is to follow this plan, get married and so phrase my will that Hubert cannot get his hands on the King money.

"That is the reason for the sacrifice you are making, Randi. Your part in it I know. That you will be a gallant and sunny-hearted wife, without bitterness and disloyalty, I know too. But I believe, I am fairly sure from my talks with my physician, that the ordeal will not be a long one. In a few months, perhaps a year at most, you will be free. When that time comes, I do not want you to grieve for me. I want you to have the full, joyous, fulfilled life of a woman with the husband she loves and children around her. I rather imagine, since my house is to be Cary's, as director of the King Foundation, that this is the home you will bless and make radiant. I would like to think of you here, keeping sunlight in the rooms.

"But whoever the man may be whom you will enrich with your love, and you will do that wholeheartedly as you do everything, I want to thank you for the happiness you are bringing me. And now — as I can do so without causing you any pain or obligation — I must tell you one more thing. I love you, Randi. You bring me all the happiness I have ever known. Be happy, my darling. Be very happy. Jonas."

After a long time Randi dried her eyes and put the

letter gently away. Then she pulled on boots and a warm car coat with a hood and woolen gloves and went out into the gray day, looking for signs of spring.

She found herself walking, as she had walked so many times, along Main Street, past the building on which Mr. Echo had worked, and which was now renting office space above and store space below, past the corner where she had stopped so often in the hope of catching a glimpse of Willis as he went in and out of his office, up the hill that led to the big estates, past the high wall and through the open gates and up the gravel driveway to the door of Jonas's house.

Vaguely she told herself that she was going to call on Hal and Sally and find out how the new book was going. But there was a car outside the house, a rather ancient Renault, and suddenly Randi's heart was tumbling, racing, skipping, making a tumult in her veins.

The front door opened and Luther came out, removed suitcases and typewriter from the trunk of the little car, caught sight of her standing there, head down because of the force of the wind.

"Mrs. King!" His face lighted up. She took a hesitant step forward. "Mr. Hamilton has just arrived." He gestured toward the front door. "He'll be so glad —"

Randi found herself shaking her head. "Oh, no!" she said. She turned, ran blindly down the driveway toward the gates and the street beyond. And behind her there were pounding feet.

"Randi!" Cary had caught her arm, turned her toward him. "Randi!"

She started to pull away, her foot slipped on ice under the light snow. His hand tightened on her arm.

"You haven't got a coat," she heard herself saying crossly. "Go back to the house. You'll catch your death of cold."

And then the face that had looked so grim, so forbidding, was altered as he broke into laughter. "Quite probably," he agreed. "So you had better come in and save my life. Because," as she did not move, "I'm not going alone. Not without you. Not ever again."

She was going with him now, submissive to his hand on her arm. They were in the great drawing room where she had been married. He steered her back to the smaller living room where a fire blazed on the hearth.

He took her car coat and flung it over a chair, knelt beside her to draw off her boots. Still on his knees he said, "I guess this is the best position I could be in, Randi," and there was no more laughter in him, "to beg your pardon from my heart. To tell you how bitterly I have regretted the things I said, my lack of faith in you. And yet all the time I —"

His hand was warm on her ankle. "Is it too much to ask you to forgive me? When I think of you risking your life, trying to protect me from that bomb, when I think —"

"Don't," she said. "Don't think about it. That's the past."

She moved her foot and he released her at once, but he did not get to his feet. "Do you mean we can start all over again?"

"Well, I —"

Now he got up quickly, moved away from her to the window. "A year ago," he said quietly, "I met you and found the girl I had wanted all my life. And then Jonas King told me that you were going to be his wife. So I was —" His voice rose for a moment in a kind of anger. "I was handcuffed and bound and gagged. I couldn't plead my cause. I couldn't speak for myself. Even if —" He shook his head helplessly and then tried again.

"Then there came all my ugly jealousy of Willis Jameson that made me distrust you. When I remember that — no wonder you can't wipe out the past."

"I don't want to wipe it out," Randi said. "The past is a part of us as well as the future."

"I haven't any future without you, Randi. For a year I've waited. I love you completely."

He had come back again, he was standing beside her chair. "I'm sorry. The moment I see you all the barriers come tumbling down and I say things I have no right to say. I've done nothing but distrust you and behave badly. You've no reason even to — to like me. So I have no right to hope —"

"Hope what?"

"Hope that you can learn to love me. Hope you will come home here as my wife."

"But Cary —" For a moment it seemed to Randi that she was not going to be able to get out the words. Then she saw his drawn face, his searching eyes. "But Cary," she said more clearly, "don't you see —"

"See what?"

"I have come home."

Luther, bringing in a tray with teapot and cups, thin brown-bread sandwiches and hot buttered toast, came to a halt in the doorway. Being a well-trained servant, he balanced the tray carefully while he beamed.

Cary held Randi in his arms, her hands on his shoulders, his lips moving over her face, her eyes and cheeks and lips. Randi's hands tightened on his shoulders.

At length he released her with a little sigh and caught sight of Luther. He laughed. "I've got news for you, Luther."

The butler grinned. "No, sir! I got the message." He set down the teatray beside Randi's chair. "Everyone in this house will rejoice to have you back. This house needs a lady to run it."

"So does this man," Cary told him. "When will you marry me, darling?"

Luther, picking up Randi's coat, went out discreetly.

"Whenever you like," Randi said. "You know — or did you know — that day you slipped the wedding ring on my finger I thought that was my real marriage. And Cary, there's no disloyalty to Jonas. He would be glad for our happiness. He — foresaw it."

Hours later Cary said regretfully, "I must take you back to the cottage. But not for long."

At the cottage he got out to unlock the door for her. The wind had died down, the sky had cleared, there was a thin sickle moon snared on the bare branches of a tree. And then in the stillness there came the shrill sound of the peepers, proclaiming loudly and exultantly the arrival of spring.

This book has been read by:-

Barbara Zahn _ _ _ _ _ January 1973